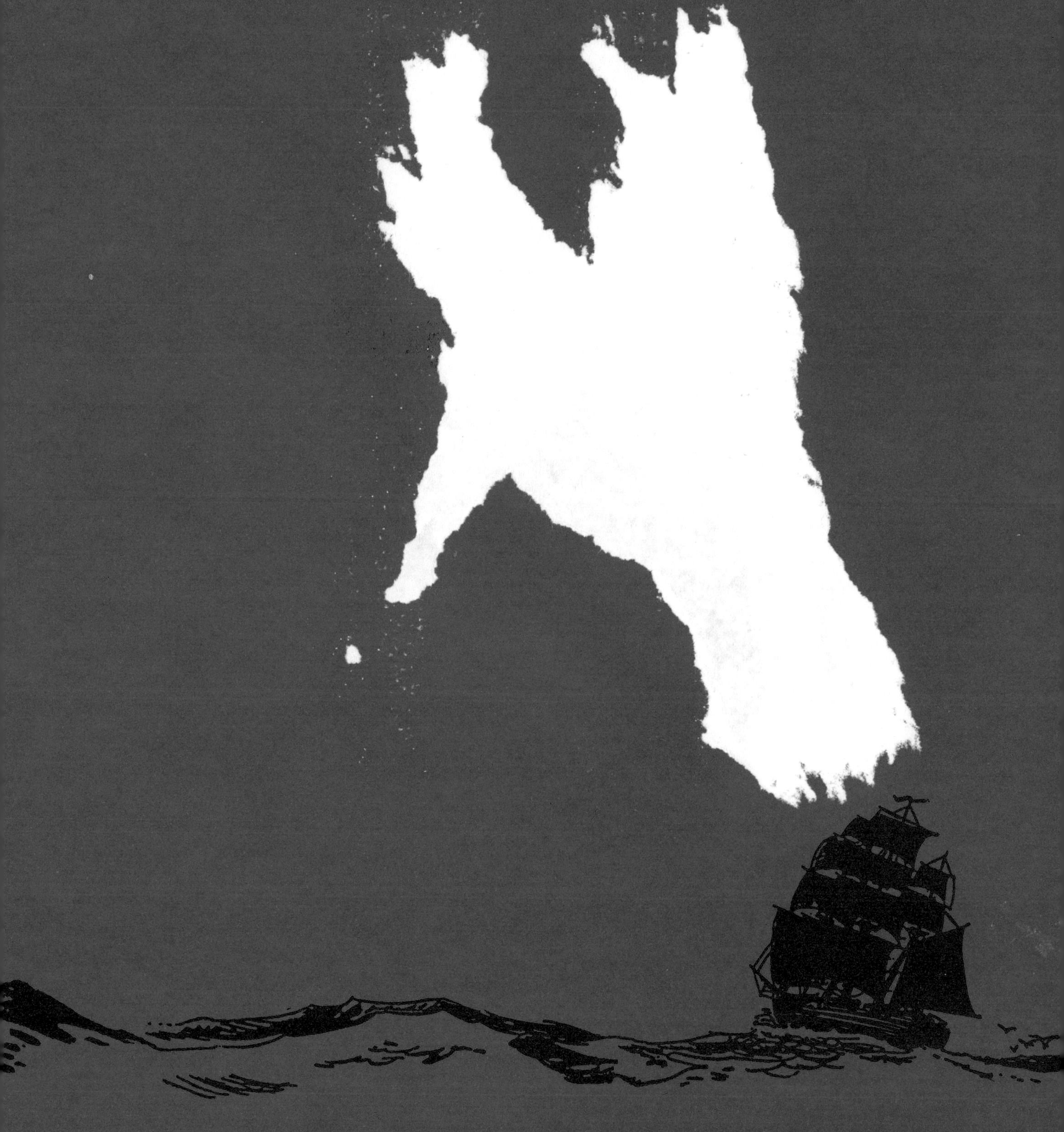

MOBY DICK

BY HERMAN MELVILLE
ADAPTED BY
Will Eisner

NANTIER · BEALL · MINOUSTCHINE
Publishing inc.
new york

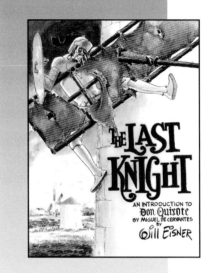

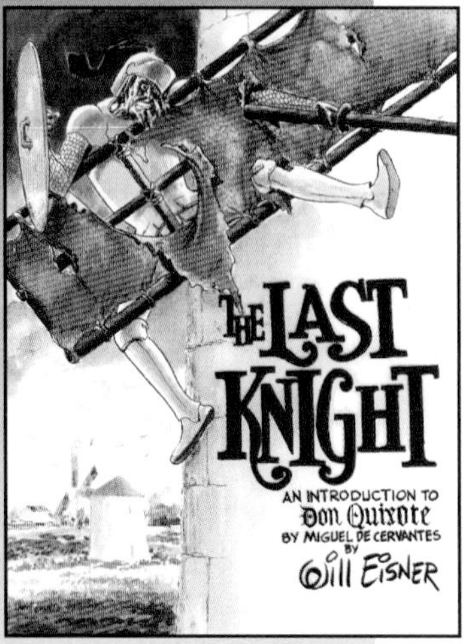
THE LAST KNIGHT
AN INTRODUCTION TO
Don Quixote
BY MIGUEL DE CERVANTES
BY
Will Eisner

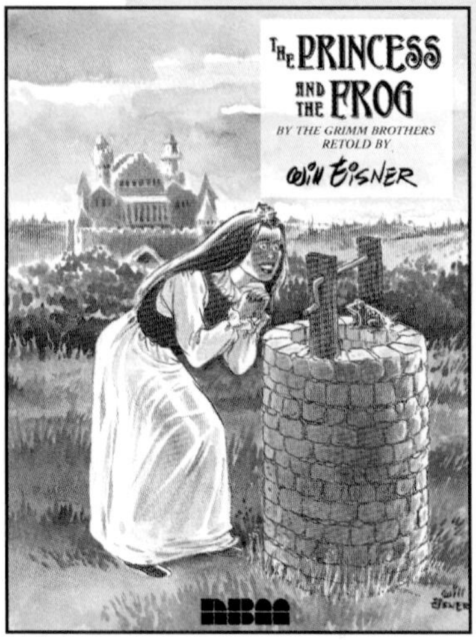
THE PRINCESS AND THE FROG
BY THE GRIMM BROTHERS
RETOLD BY
Will Eisner

ISBN 1-56163-293-7, clothbound
ISBN 1-56163-294-5, paperback
Printed in Hong Kong

5 4 3 2

Library of Congress Cataloging-in-Publication Data

Eisner, Will.
Moby Dick / by Herman Melville; adapted by Will Eisner.
p.cm.
Summary: Ishmael, a sailor, recounts the ill-fated voyage of a whaling ship led by the fanatical Captain Ahab in search of the white whale that had crippled him. Presented in comic book format.
ISBN 1-56163-293-7 (cloth) --ISBN 1-56163-294-5 (pbk.)
[1. Whaling--Fiction. 2. Whales--Fiction. 3. Sea stories. 4. Cartoons and comics.] I. Melville, Herman, 1819-1891. Moby Dick. II. Title.

PN6727.E4 M63 2001
741.5'973--dc21

2001032989

THE WHITE WHALE

IT WAS A TIME
WHEN MIGHTY WHALES
SWAM THE GREAT OCEANS
THEY WERE VALUED
FOR THEIR OIL AND BONE

SO MEN IN TALL SAILING SHIPS ROAMED THE SEAS TO HUNT THEM. BUT THE WHALES WERE A FIERCE FOE.

AND FROM THE STRUGGLE BETWEEN MAN AND WHALE CAME STORIES OF GREAT ADVENTURE.

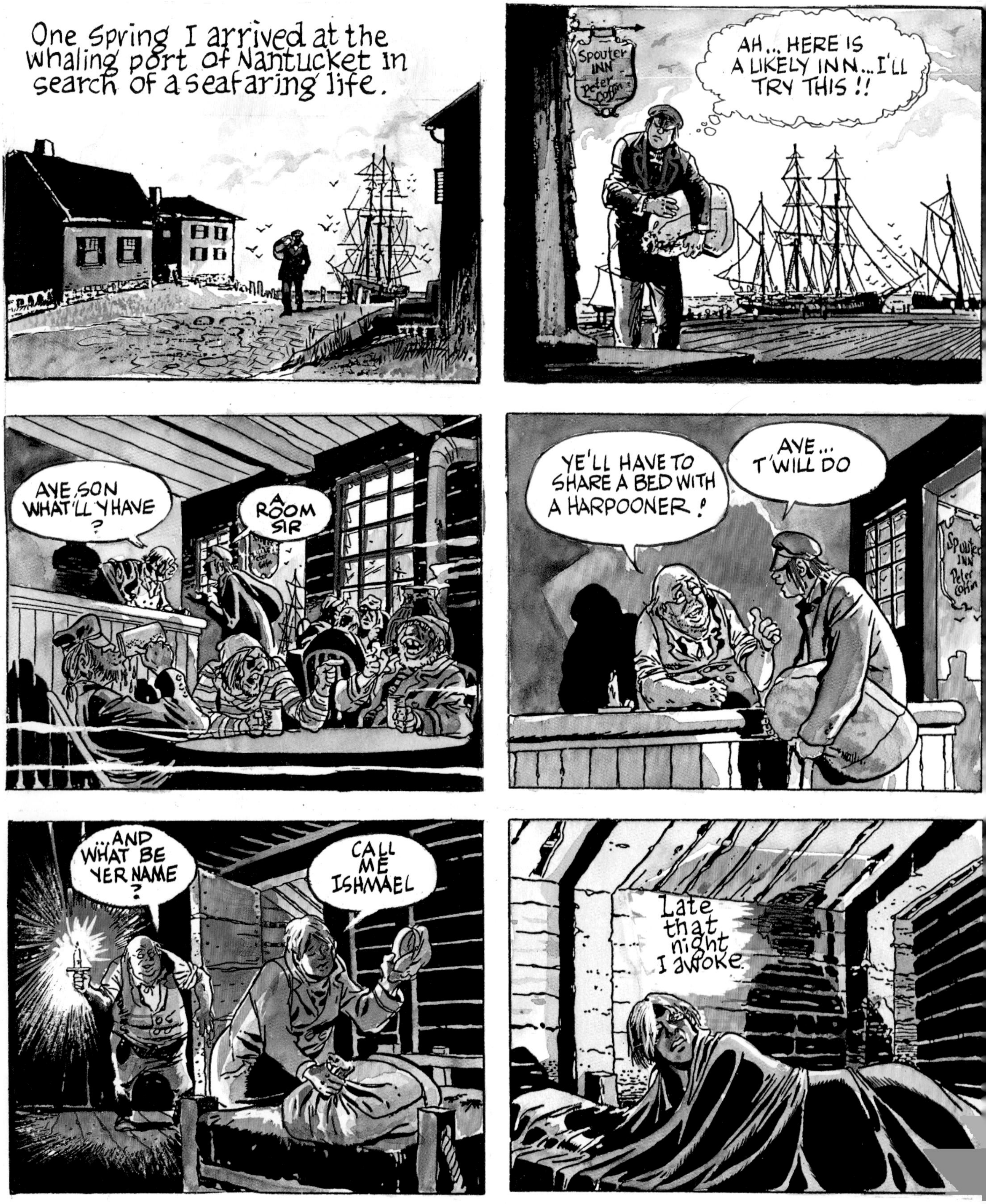
One Spring I arrived at the whaling port of Nantucket in search of a seafaring life.
Spouter INN Peter Coffin
AH... HERE IS A LIKELY INN... I'LL TRY THIS !!
AYE, SON WHAT'LL Y HAVE ?
A ROOM SIR
YE'LL HAVE TO SHARE A BED WITH A HARPOONER !
AYE... T'WILL DO
...AND WHAT BE YER NAME ?
CALL ME ISHMAEL
Late that night I awoke.

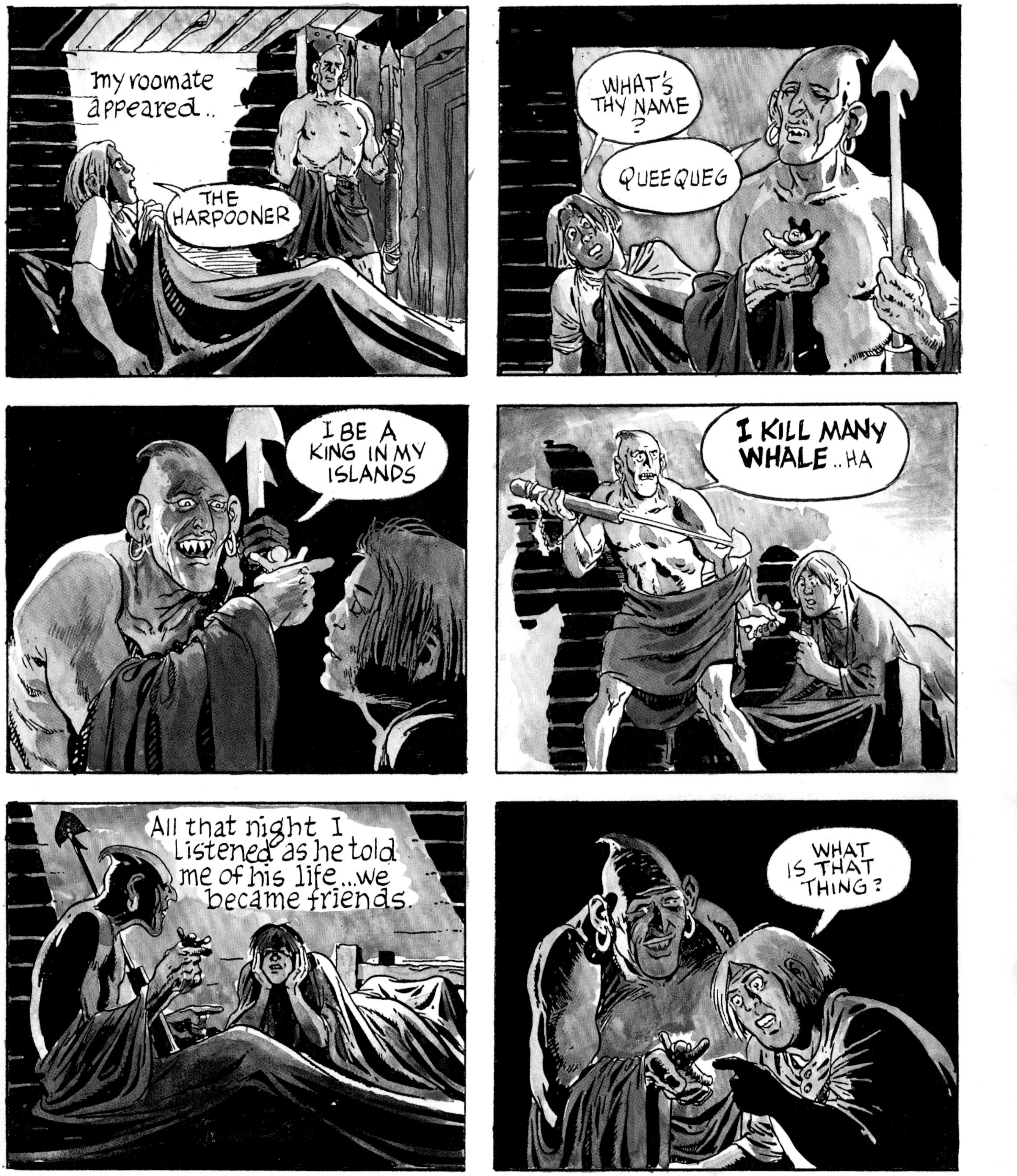
my roomate appeared..
THE HARPOONER
WHAT'S THY NAME ?
QUEEQUEG
I BE A KING IN MY ISLANDS
I KILL MANY WHALE..HA
All that night I listened as he told me of his life...we became friends.
WHAT IS THAT THING?

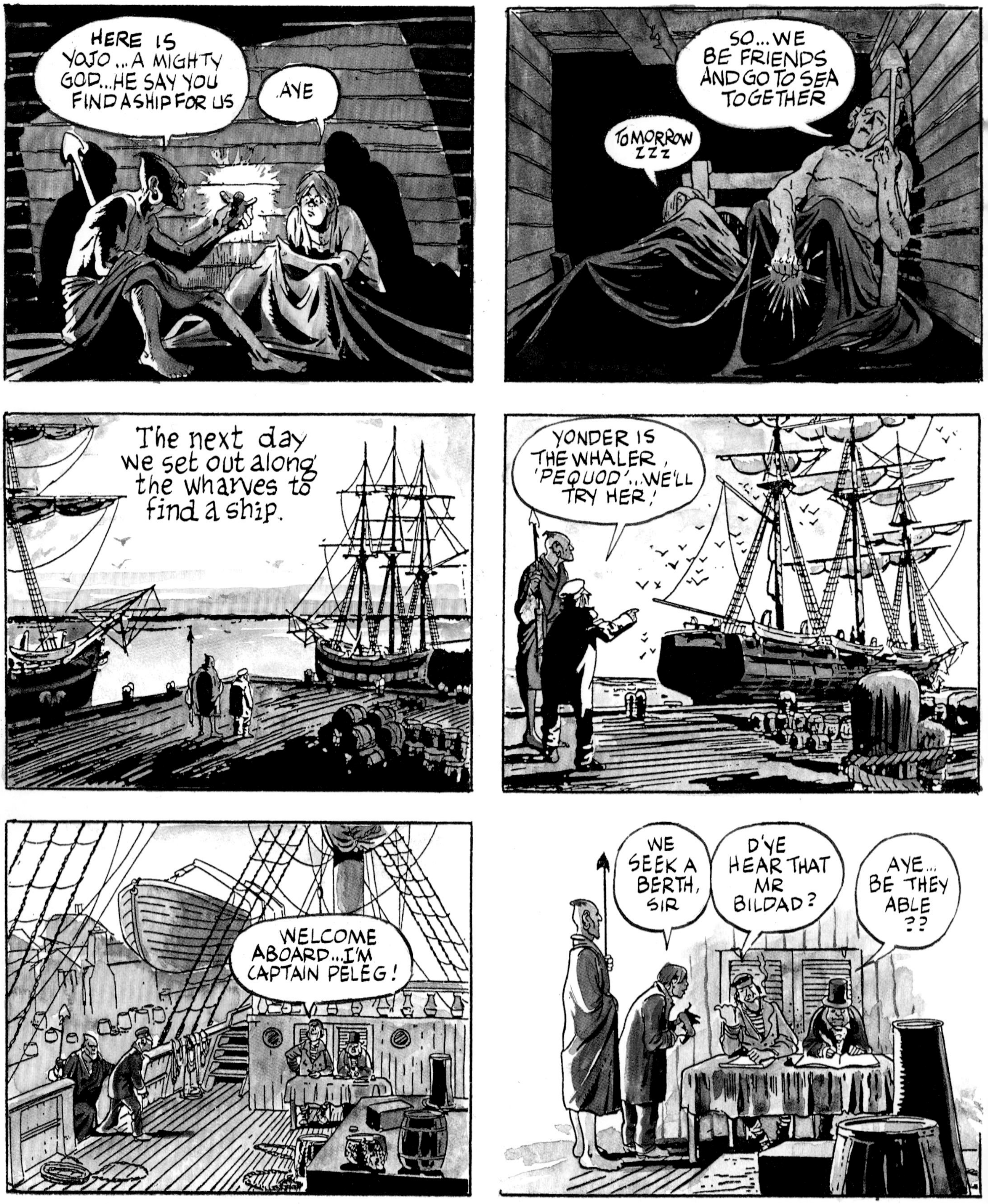
HERE IS YOJO ...A MIGHTY GOD...HE SAY YOU FIND A SHIP FOR US
AYE
SO...WE BE FRIENDS AND GO TO SEA TOGETHER
TOMORROW ZZZ
The next day we set out along the wharves to find a ship.
YONDER IS THE WHALER, 'PEQUOD'...WE'LL TRY HER!
WELCOME ABOARD...I'M CAPTAIN PELEG!
WE SEEK A BERTH, SIR
D'YE HEAR THAT MR BILDAD?
AYE... BE THEY ABLE ??

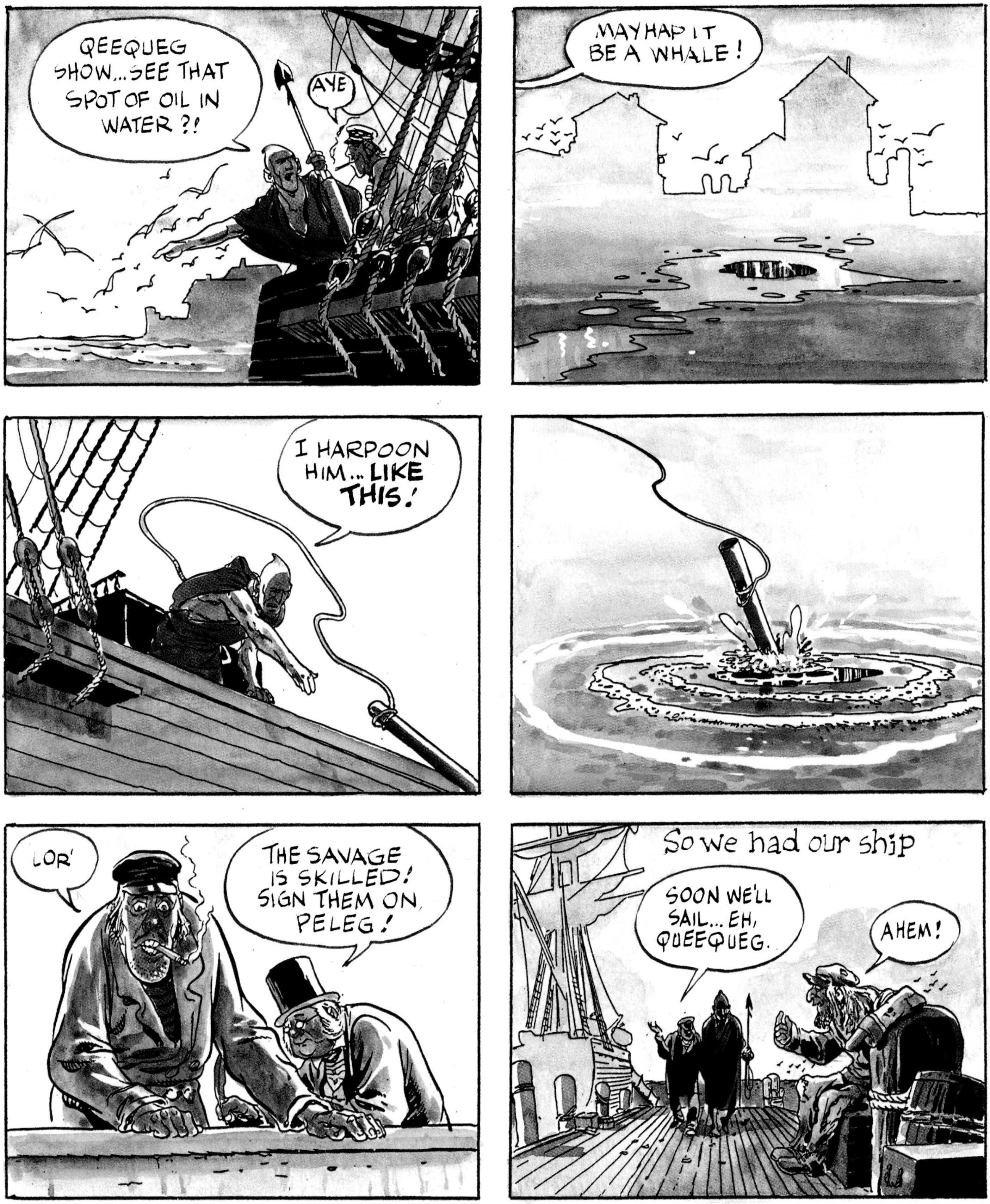
QEEQUEG SHOW... SEE THAT SPOT OF OIL IN WATER ?!
AYE
MAYHAP IT BE A WHALE!
I HARPOON HIM... **LIKE THIS!**
LOR'
THE SAVAGE IS SKILLED! SIGN THEM ON, PELEG!
So we had our ship
SOON WE'LL SAIL... EH, QUEEQUEG.
AHEM!

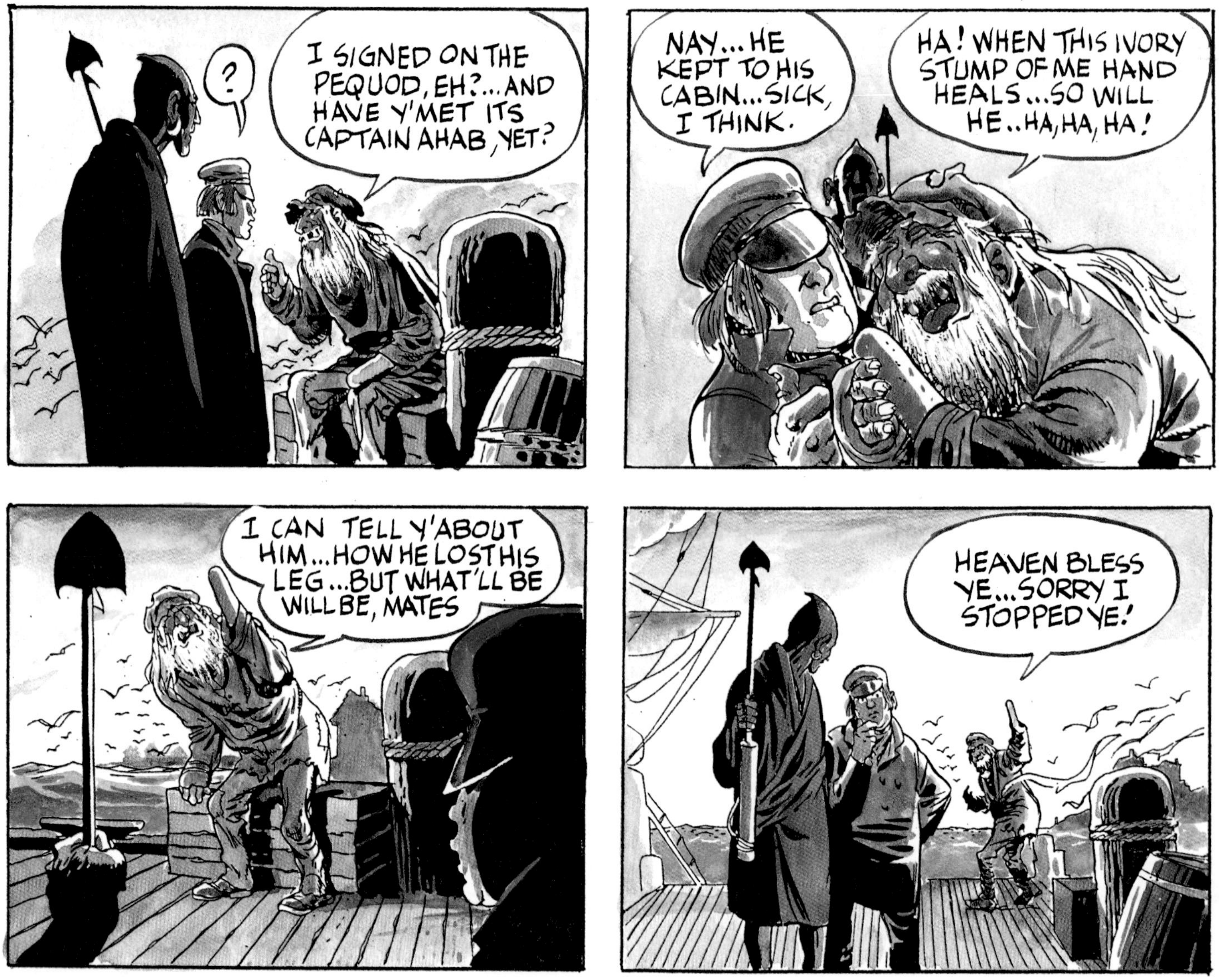
?
I SIGNED ON THE PEQUOD, EH?... AND HAVE Y'MET ITS CAPTAIN AHAB, YET?
NAY... HE KEPT TO HIS CABIN... SICK, I THINK.
HA! WHEN THIS IVORY STUMP OF ME HAND HEALS... SO WILL HE.. HA, HA, HA!
I CAN TELL Y'ABOUT HIM... HOW HE LOST HIS LEG... BUT WHAT'LL BE WILL BE, MATES
HEAVEN BLESS YE... SORRY I STOPPED YE!

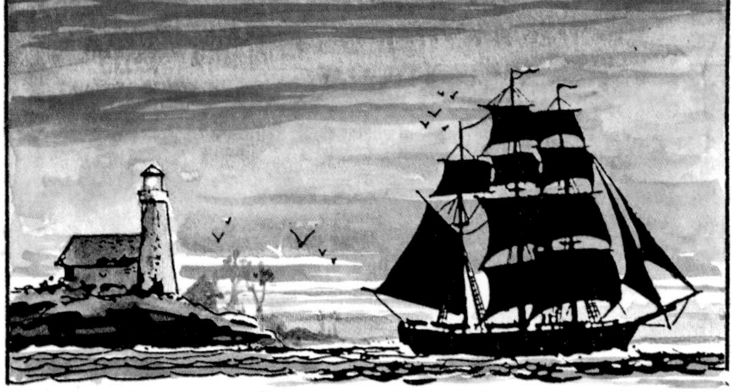

And so a few days later we put out to sea aboard the good ship Pequod.

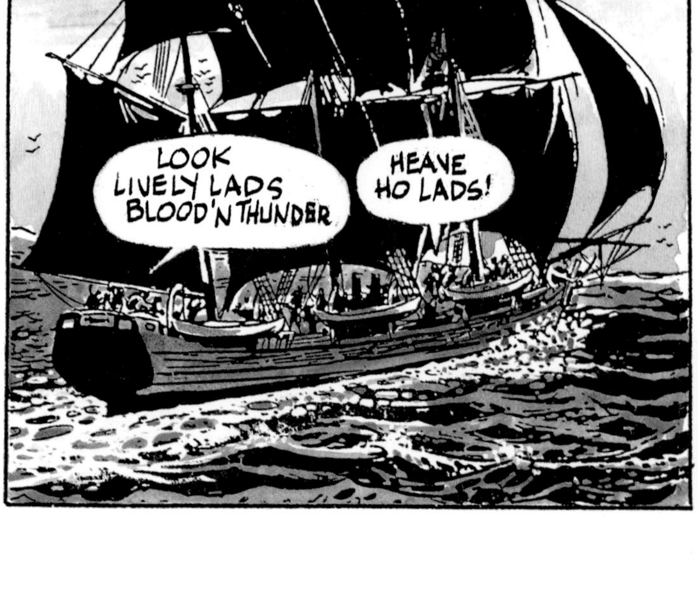
LOOK LIVELY LADS BLOOD'N THUNDER
HEAVE HO LADS!

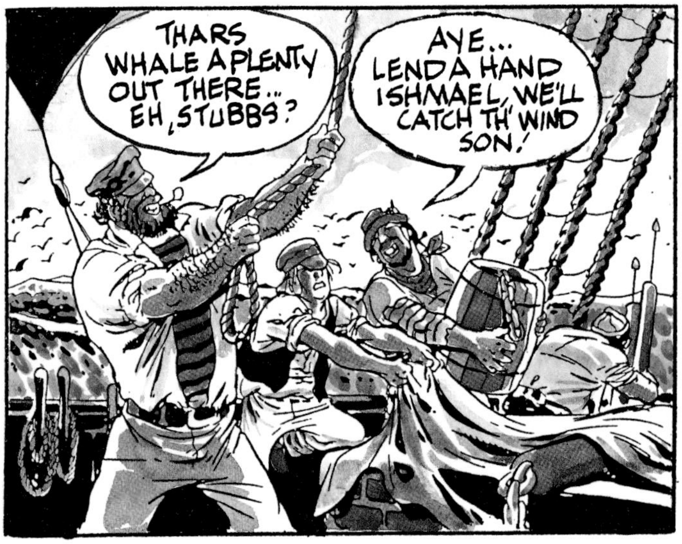
THARS WHALE APLENTY OUT THERE... EH, STUBBS?
AYE... LEND A HAND ISHMAEL, WE'LL CATCH TH' WIND SON!

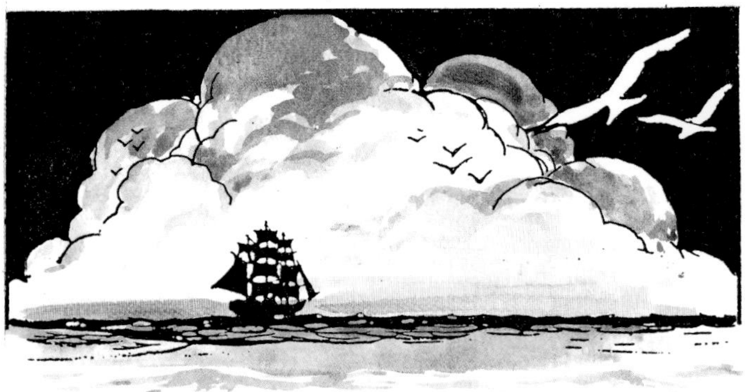

Ahead were the great oceans ... and the unknown.

Before us swam the sea creatures. Did they know of their fate I wondered.

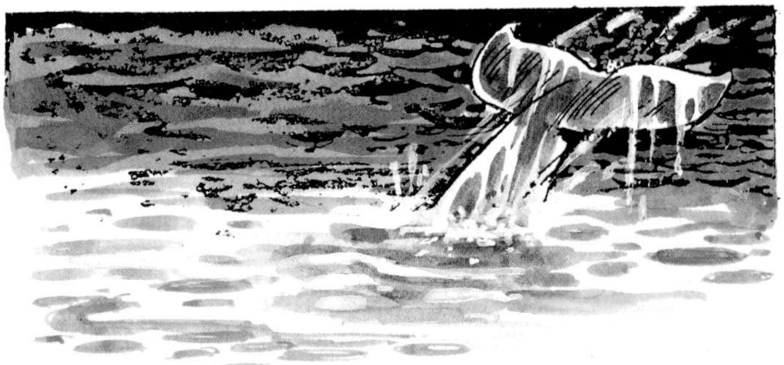

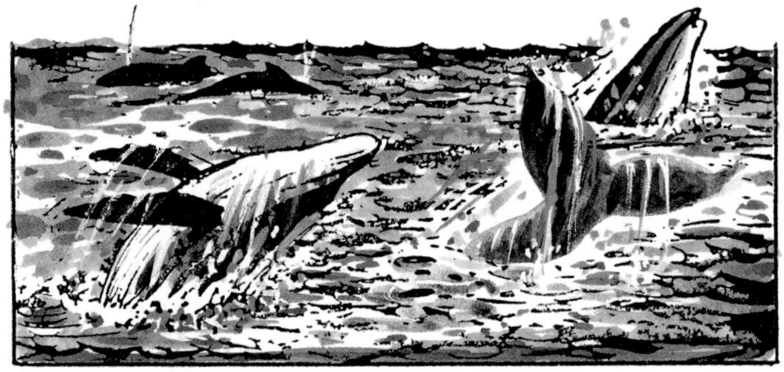

But, one did know of our coming... a great white whale, He lurked in wait.

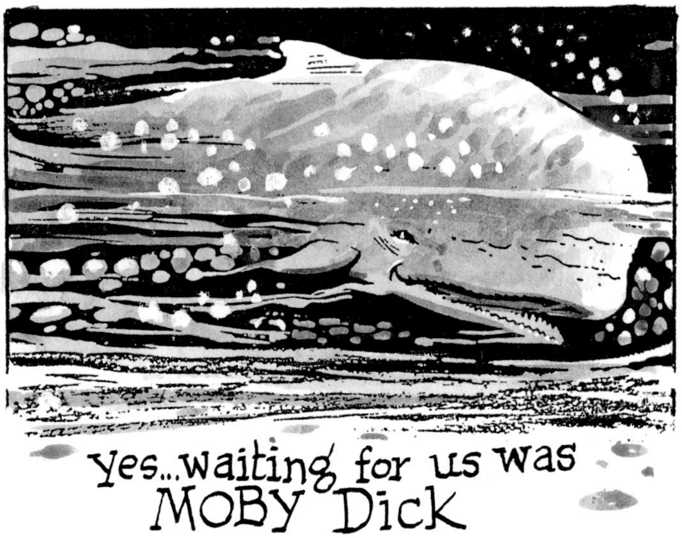

Yes...waiting for us was MOBY DICK

Around him the seas roiled and the sea birds gathered.

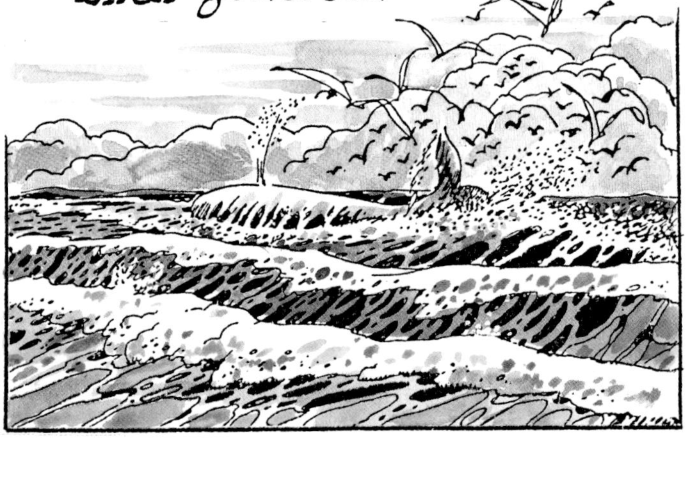

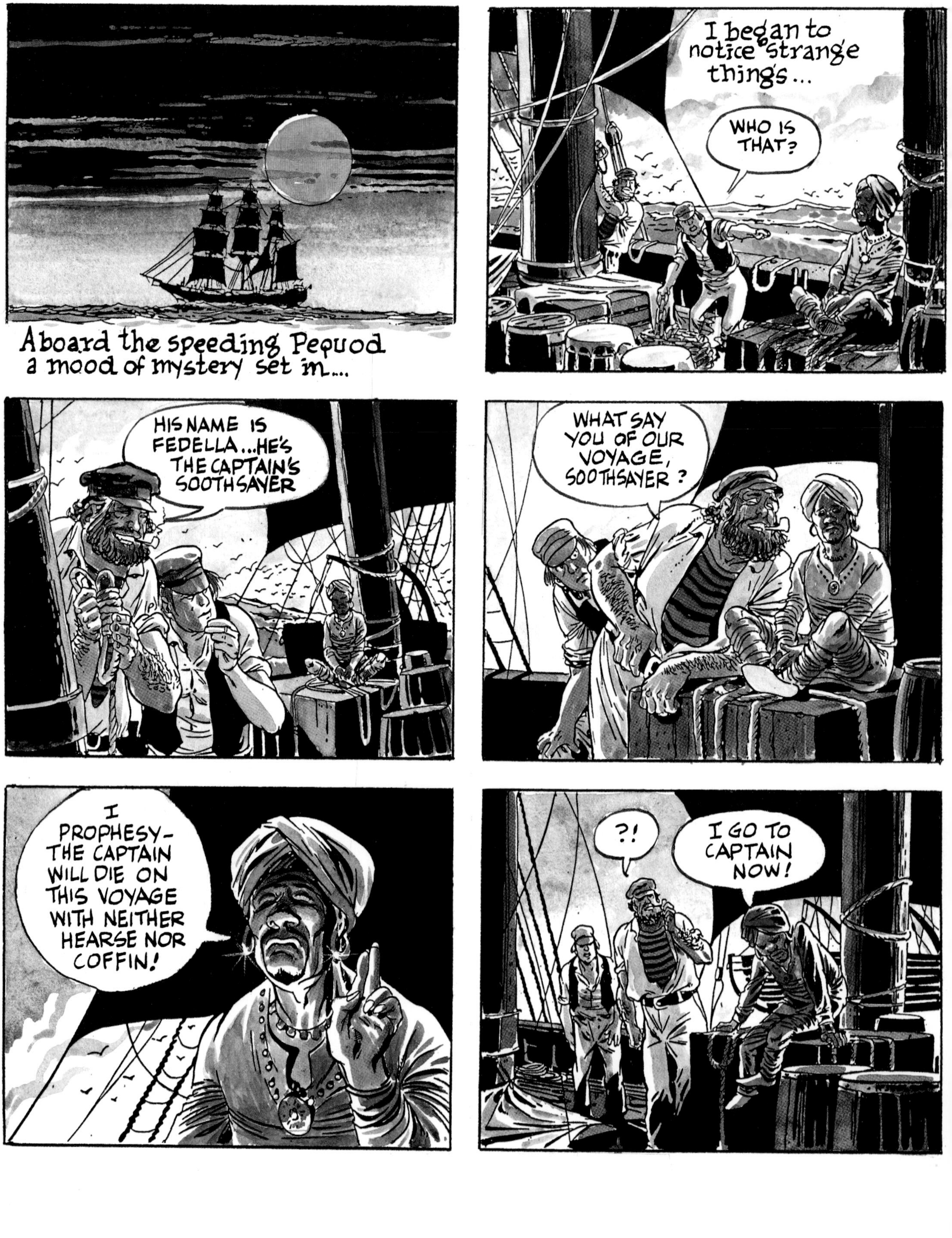
Aboard the speeding Pequod a mood of mystery set in....
I began to notice strange things...
WHO IS THAT?
HIS NAME IS FEDELLA...HE'S THE CAPTAIN'S SOOTHSAYER
WHAT SAY YOU OF OUR VOYAGE, SOOTHSAYER ?
I PROPHESY- THE CAPTAIN WILL DIE ON THIS VOYAGE WITH NEITHER HEARSE NOR COFFIN!
?!
I GO TO CAPTAIN NOW!

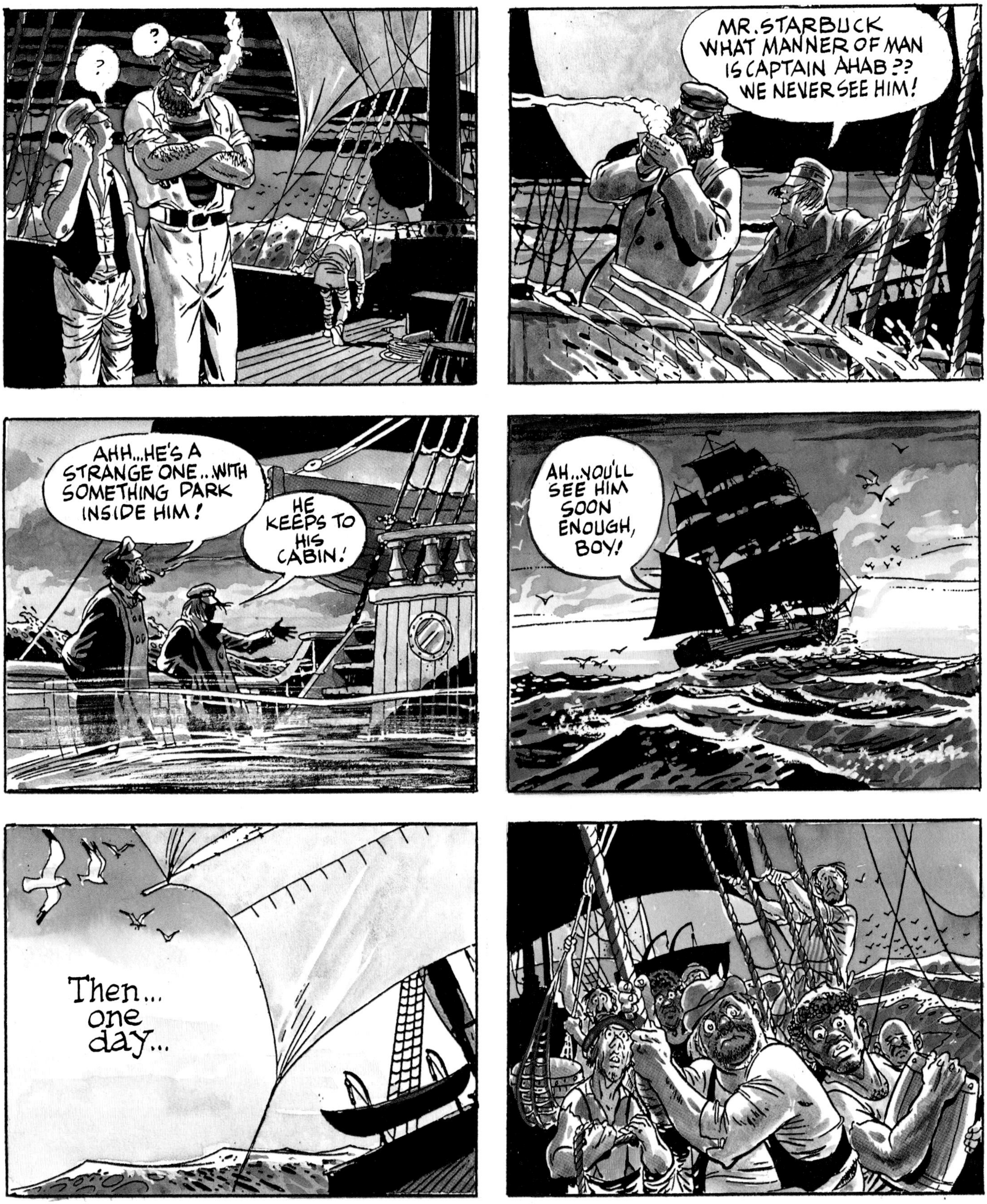
?
?
MR. STARBUCK WHAT MANNER OF MAN IS CAPTAIN AHAB ?? WE NEVER SEE HIM!
AHH...HE'S A STRANGE ONE...WITH SOMETHING DARK INSIDE HIM!
HE KEEPS TO HIS CABIN!
AH...YOU'LL SEE HIM SOON ENOUGH, BOY!
Then... one day...

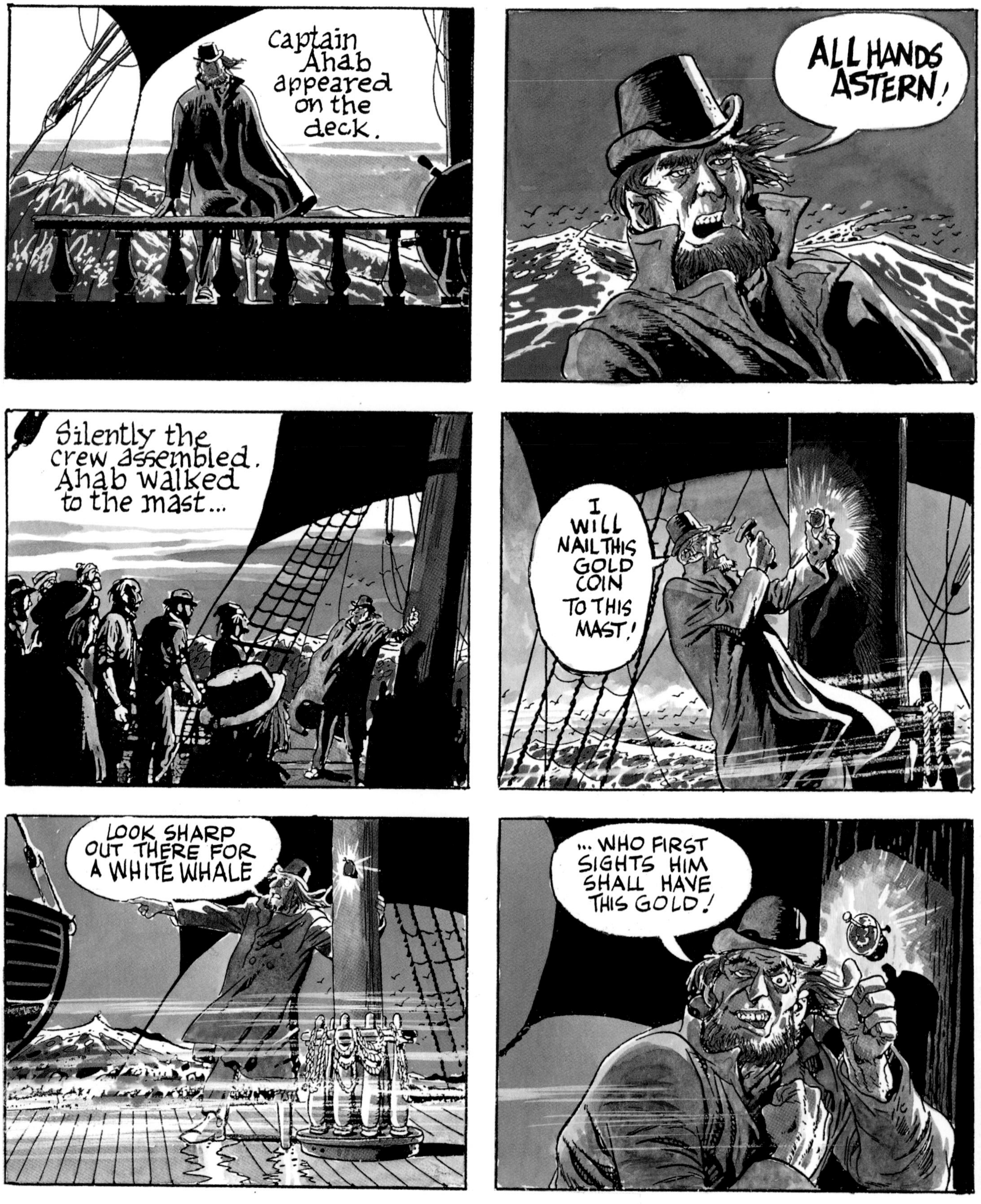
Captain Ahab appeared on the deck.
ALL HANDS ASTERN!
Silently the crew assembled. Ahab walked to the mast...
I WILL NAIL THIS GOLD COIN TO THIS MAST!
LOOK SHARP OUT THERE FOR A WHITE WHALE
... WHO FIRST SIGHTS HIM SHALL HAVE THIS GOLD!

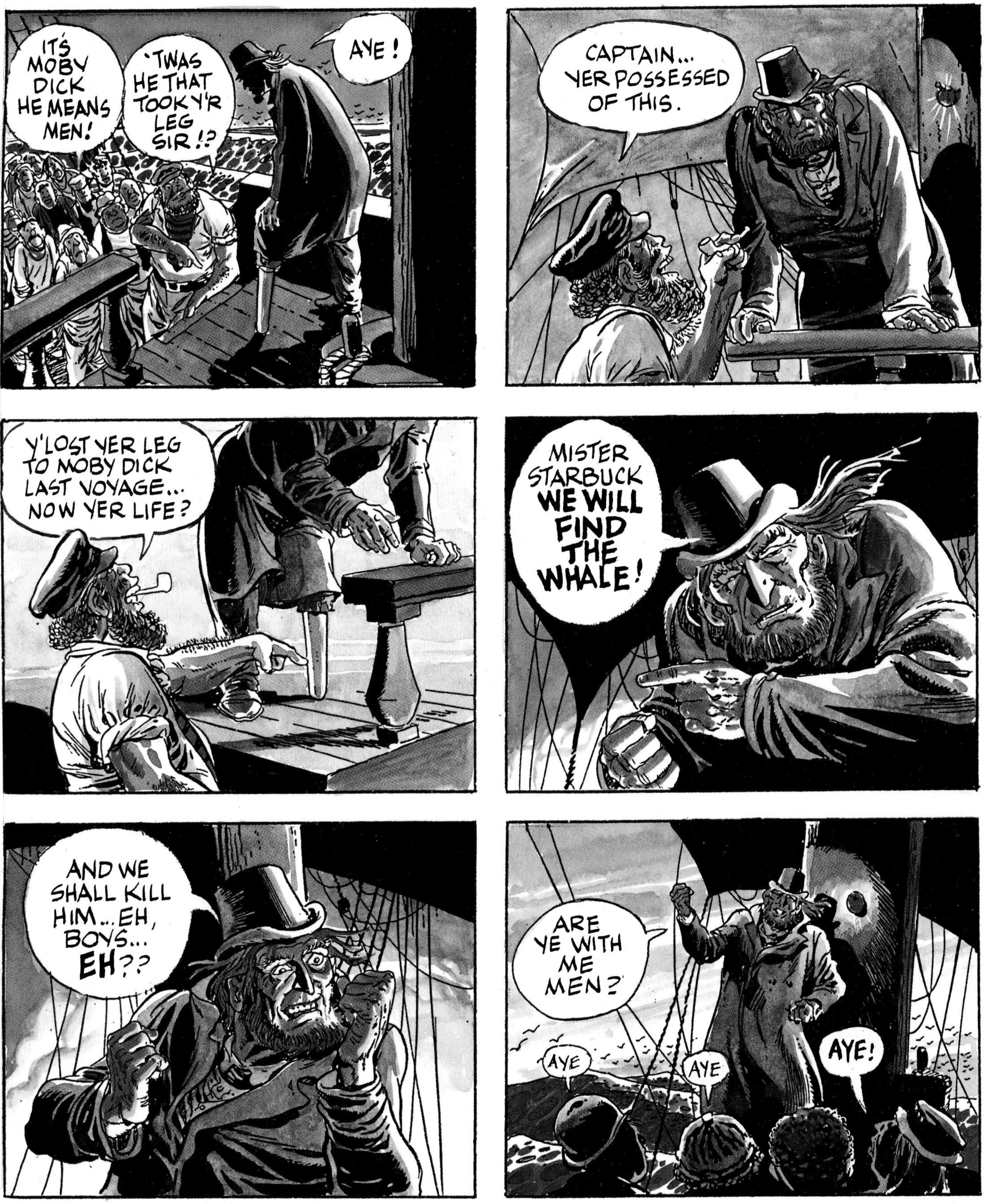
IT'S MOBY DICK HE MEANS MEN!
'TWAS HE THAT TOOK Y'R LEG SIR!?
AYE!
CAPTAIN... YER POSSESSED OF THIS.
Y'LOST YER LEG TO MOBY DICK LAST VOYAGE... NOW YER LIFE?
MISTER STARBUCK WE WILL FIND THE WHALE!
AND WE SHALL KILL HIM...EH, BOYS... EH??
ARE YE WITH ME MEN?
AYE
AYE
AYE!

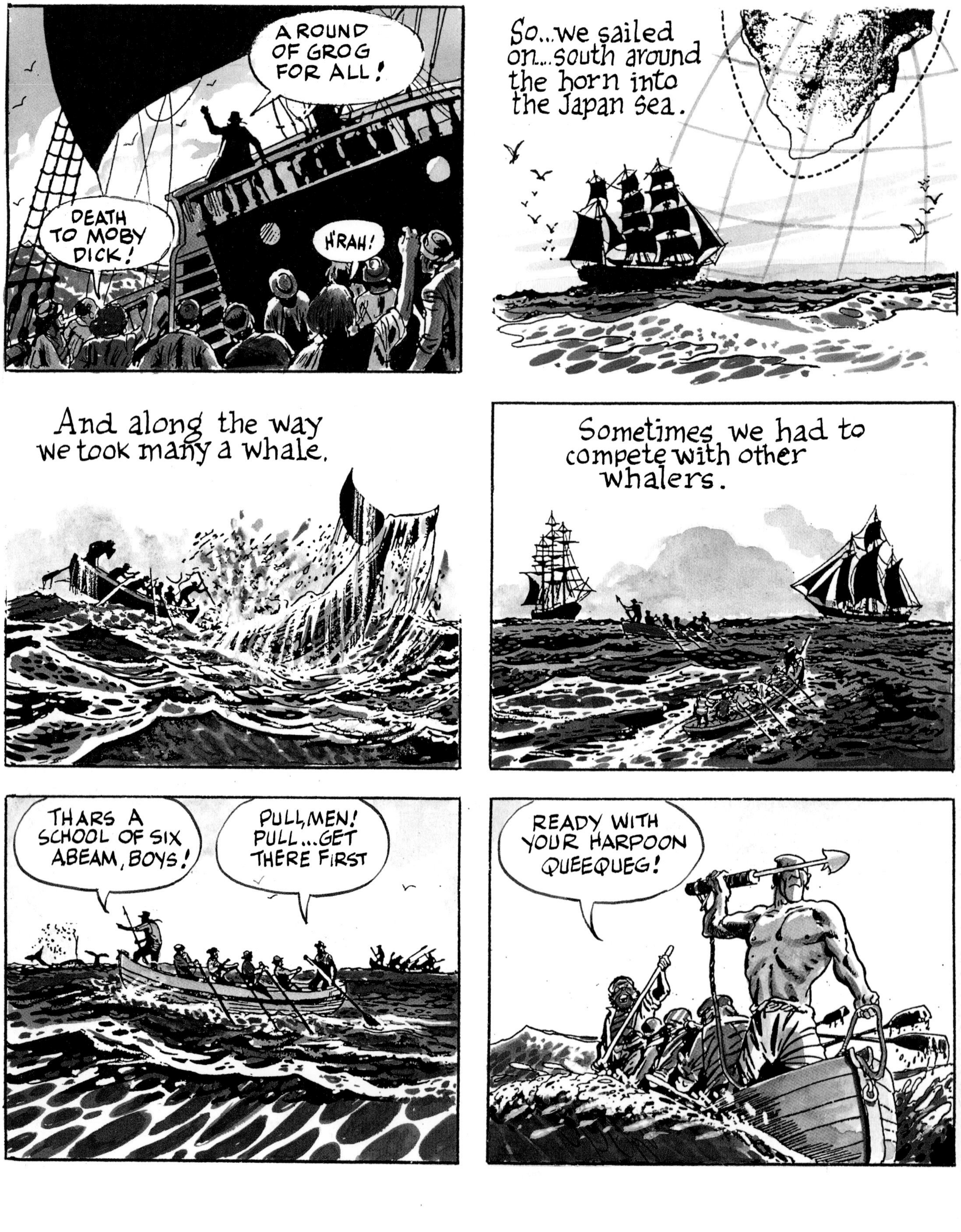
A ROUND OF GROG FOR ALL!
DEATH TO MOBY DICK!
H'RAH!
So...we sailed on...south around the horn into the Japan sea.
And along the way we took many a whale.
Sometimes we had to compete with other whalers.
THARS A SCHOOL OF SIX ABEAM, BOYS!
PULL, MEN! PULL...GET THERE FIRST
READY WITH YOUR HARPOON QUEEQUEG!

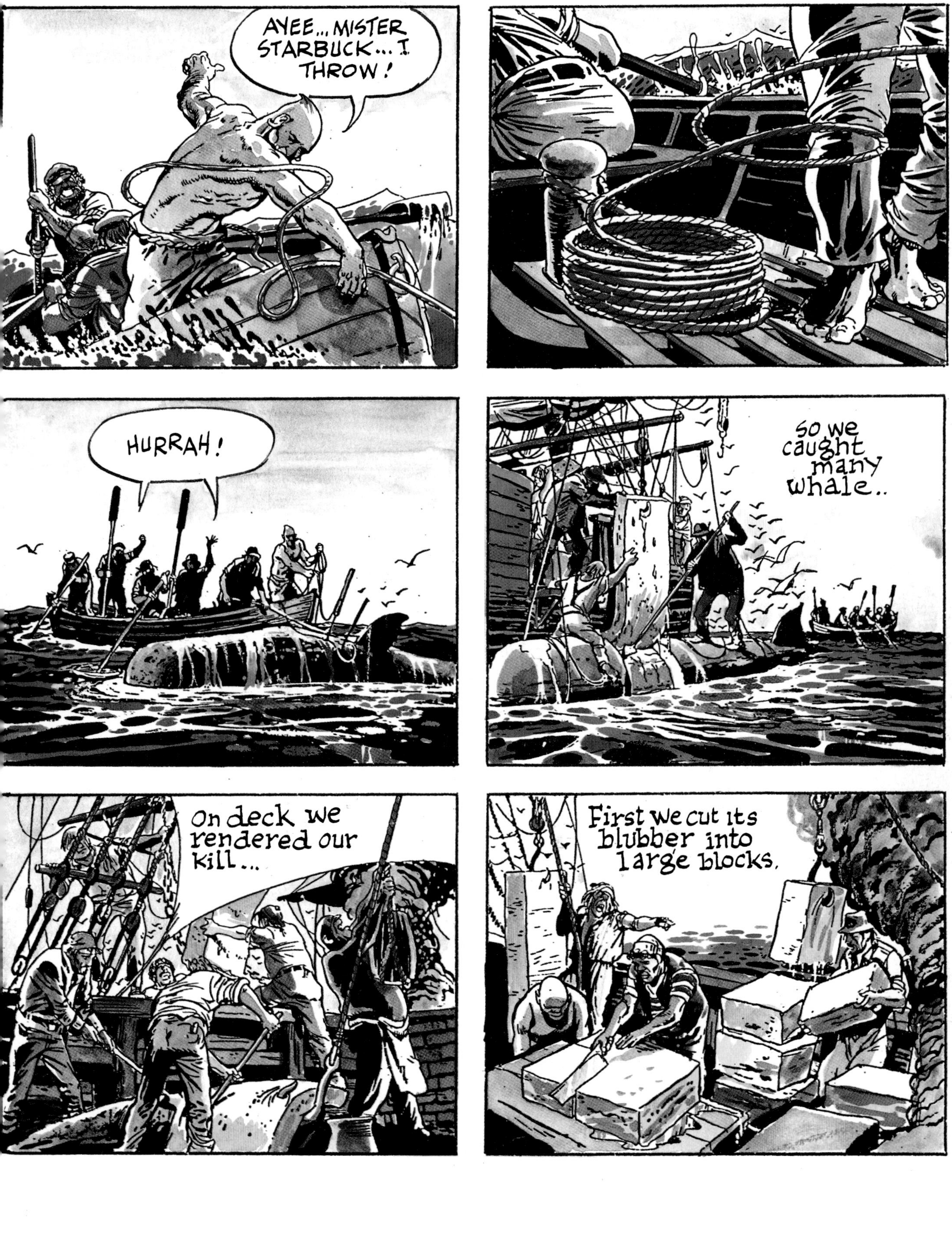
AYEE... MISTER STARBUCK... I THROW!
HURRAH!
so we caught many whale..
On deck we rendered our kill...
First we cut its blubber into large blocks.

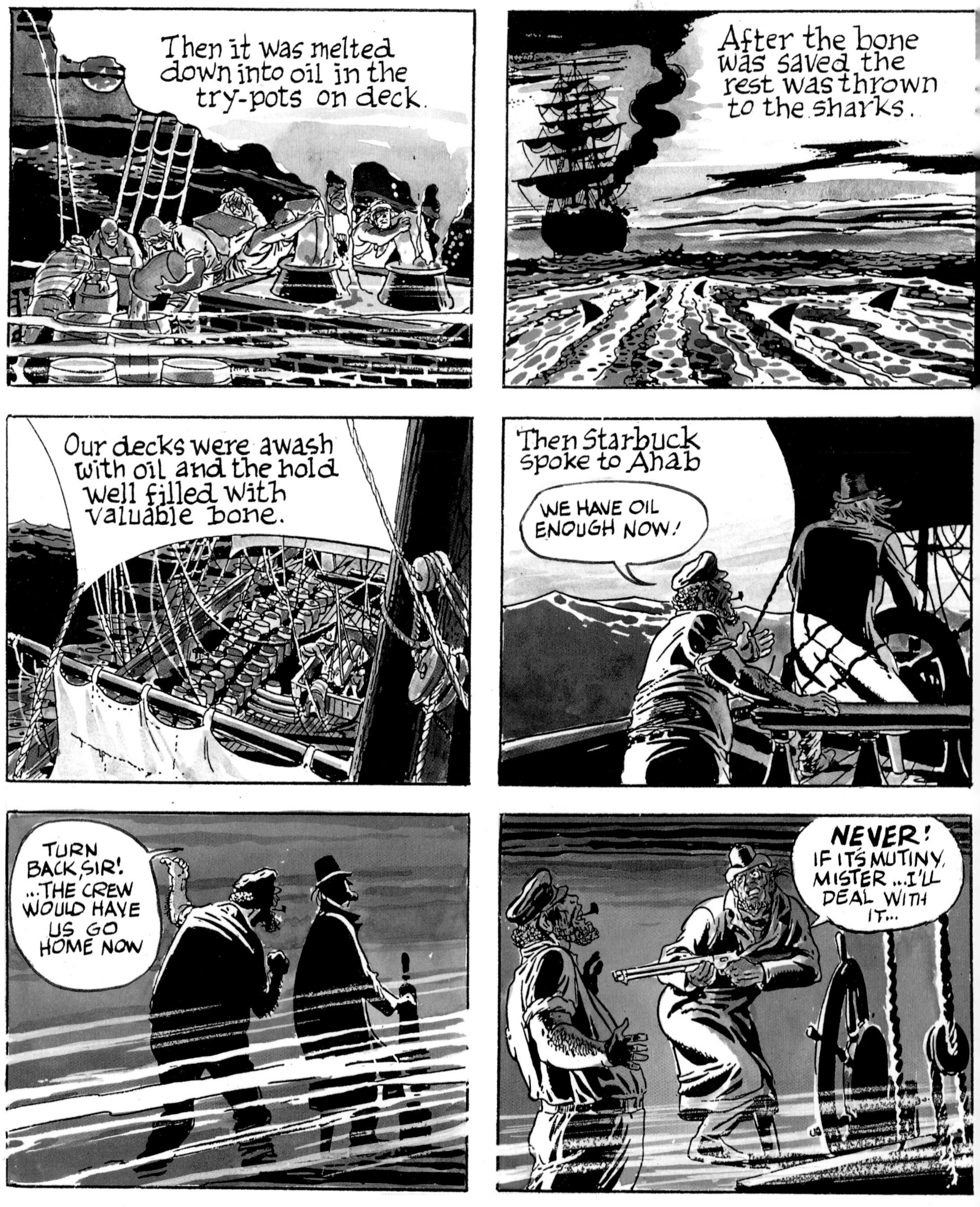
Then it was melted down into oil in the try-pots on deck.
After the bone was saved the rest was thrown to the sharks.
Our decks were awash with oil and the hold well filled with valuable bone.
Then Starbuck spoke to Ahab
WE HAVE OIL ENOUGH NOW!
TURN BACK, SIR! ...THE CREW WOULD HAVE US GO HOME NOW
NEVER! IF IT'S MUTINY, MISTER ...I'LL DEAL WITH IT...

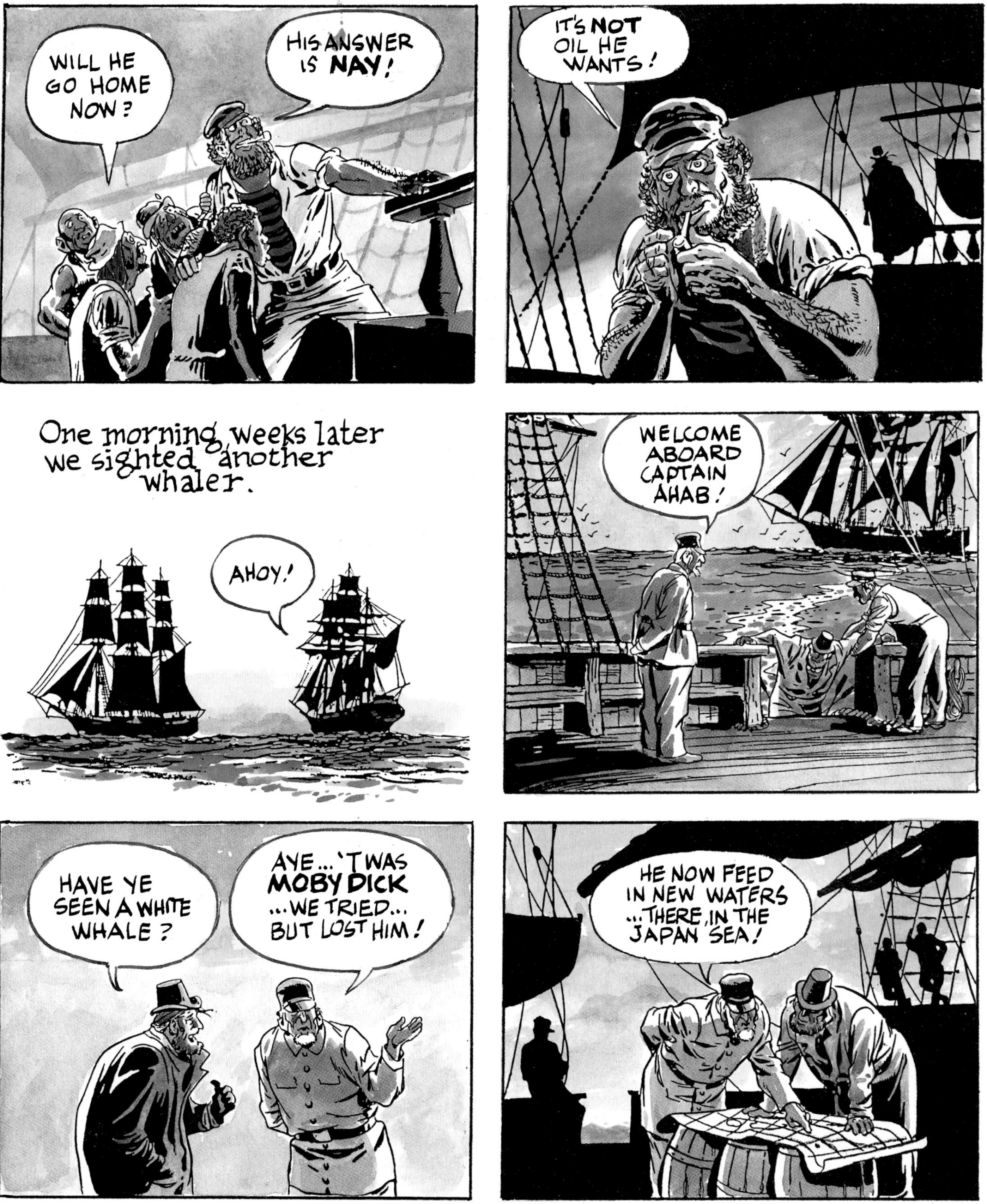
WILL HE GO HOME NOW?
HIS ANSWER IS NAY!
IT'S NOT OIL HE WANTS!
One morning weeks later we sighted another whaler.
AHOY!
WELCOME ABOARD CAPTAIN AHAB!
HAVE YE SEEN A WHITE WHALE?
AYE... 'TWAS MOBY DICK ...WE TRIED... BUT LOST HIM!
HE NOW FEED IN NEW WATERS ...THERE, IN THE JAPAN SEA!

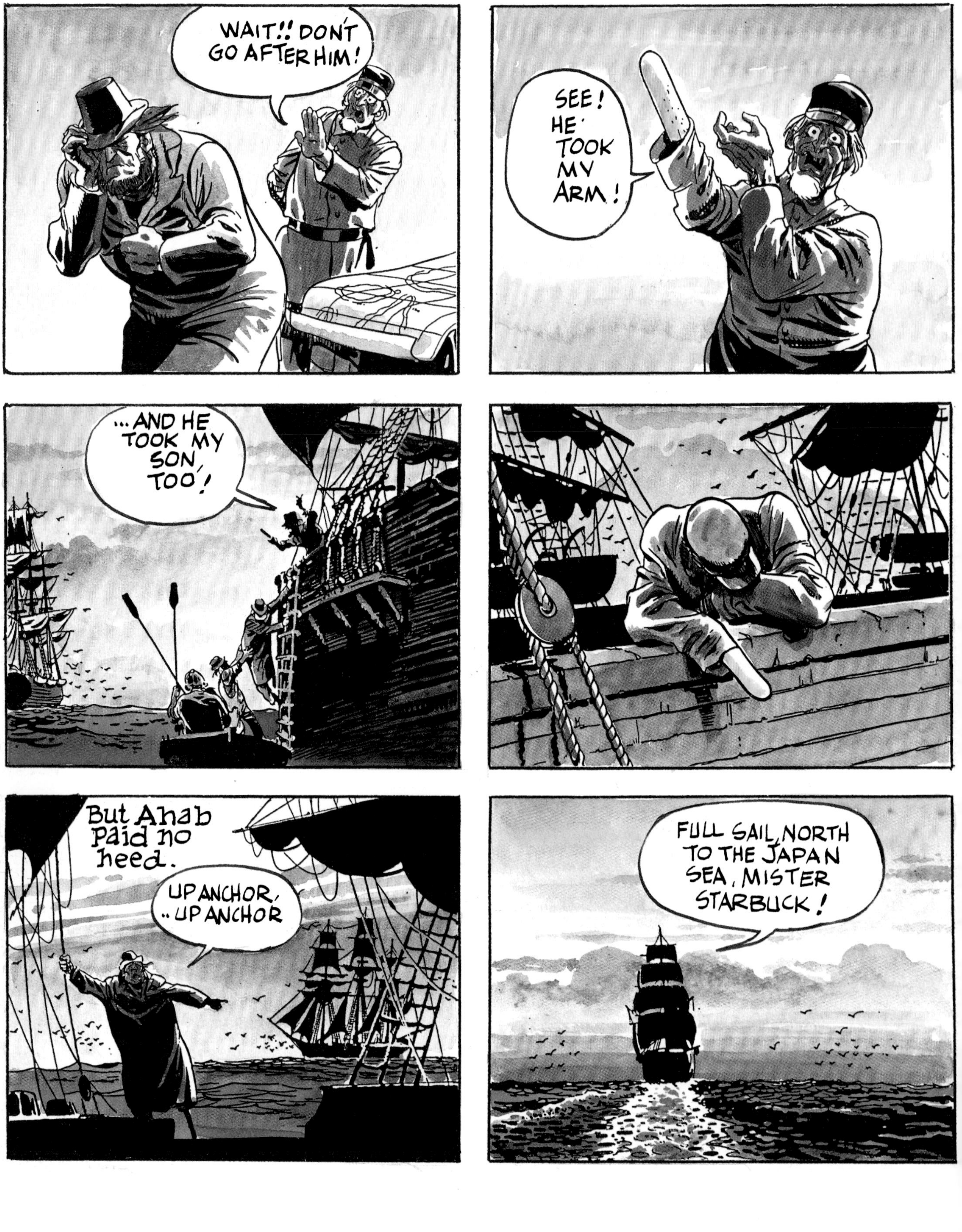
WAIT!! DON'T GO AFTER HIM!
SEE! HE TOOK MY ARM!
...AND HE TOOK MY SON, TOO!
But Ahab paid no heed.
UP ANCHOR, .. UP ANCHOR
FULL SAIL, NORTH TO THE JAPAN SEA, MISTER STARBUCK!

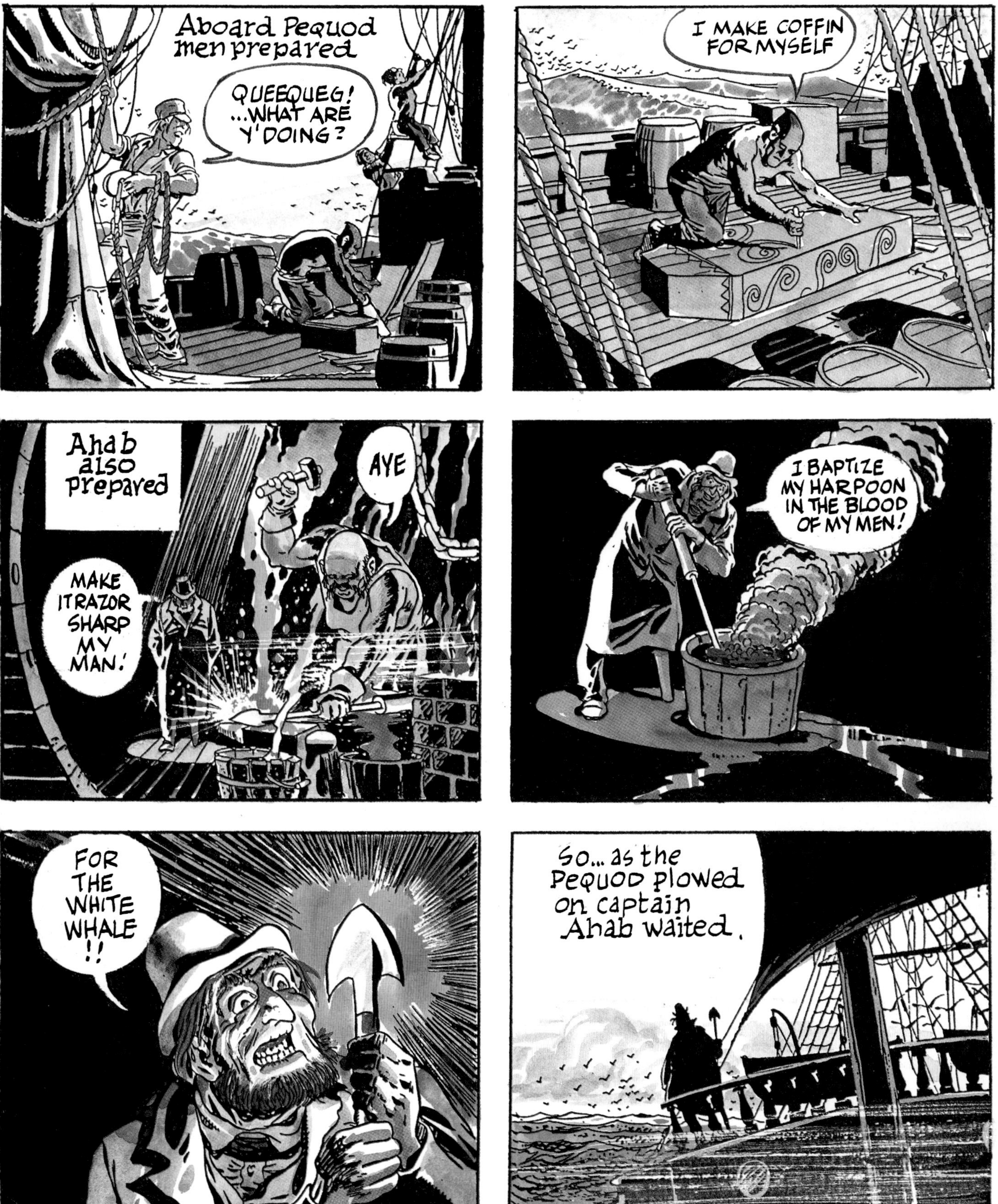
Aboard Pequod men prepared
QUEEQUEG! ...WHAT ARE Y'DOING?
I MAKE COFFIN FOR MYSELF
Ahab also prepared
AYE
MAKE IT RAZOR SHARP MY MAN!
I BAPTIZE MY HARPOON IN THE BLOOD OF MY MEN!
FOR THE WHITE WHALE !!
So... as the PEQUOD plowed on captain Ahab waited.

Ahead in the dark depths Moby Dick waited.

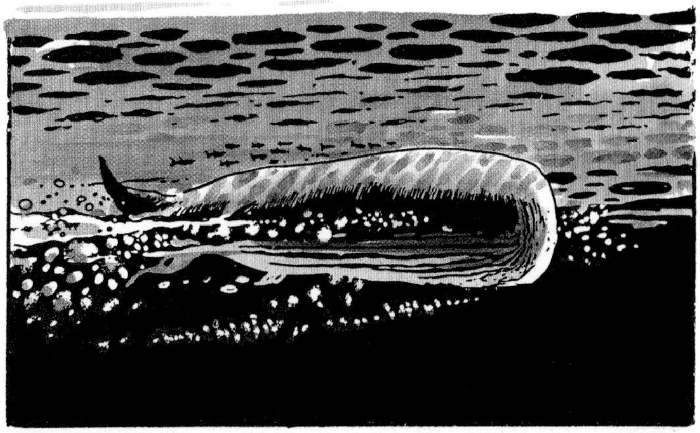

Aboard the Pequod a sense of danger seemed to push the ship onward.

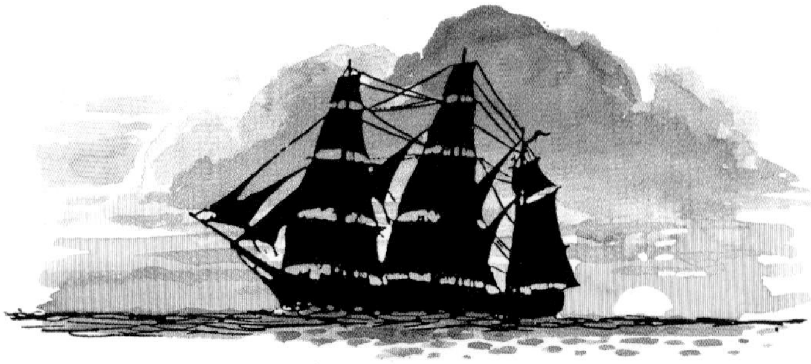

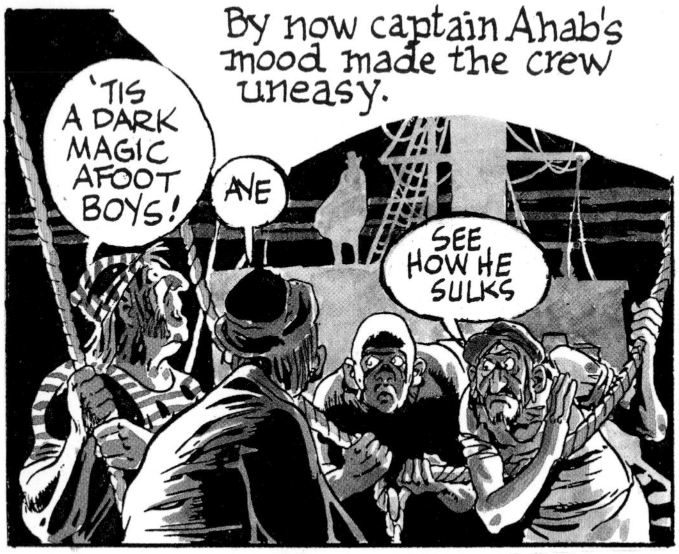
By now captain Ahab's mood made the crew uneasy.
'TIS A DARK MAGIC AFOOT BOYS!
AYE
SEE HOW HE SULKS

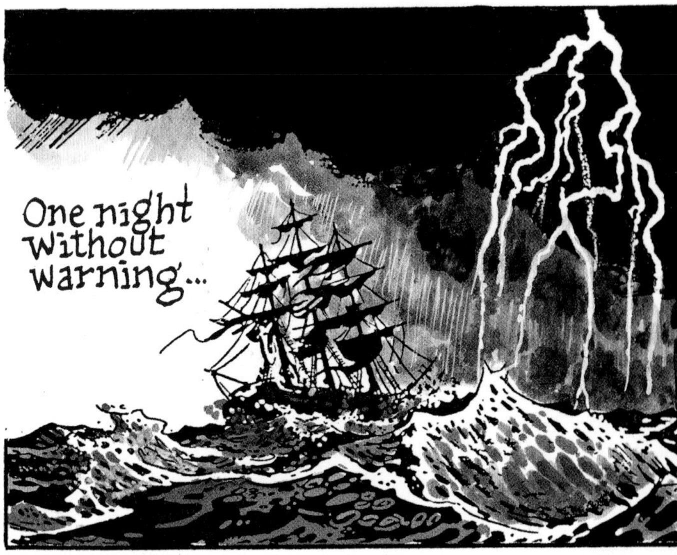
One night without warning...

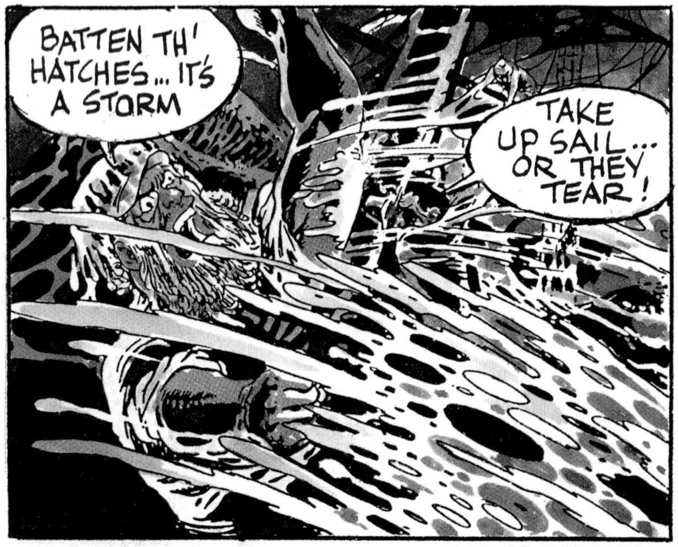
BATTEN TH' HATCHES... IT'S A STORM
TAKE UP SAIL... OR THEY TEAR!

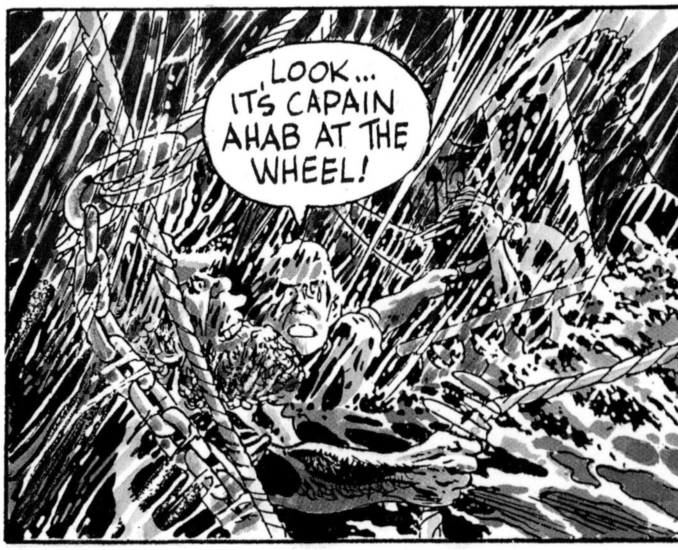
LOOK... IT'S CAPAIN AHAB AT THE WHEEL!

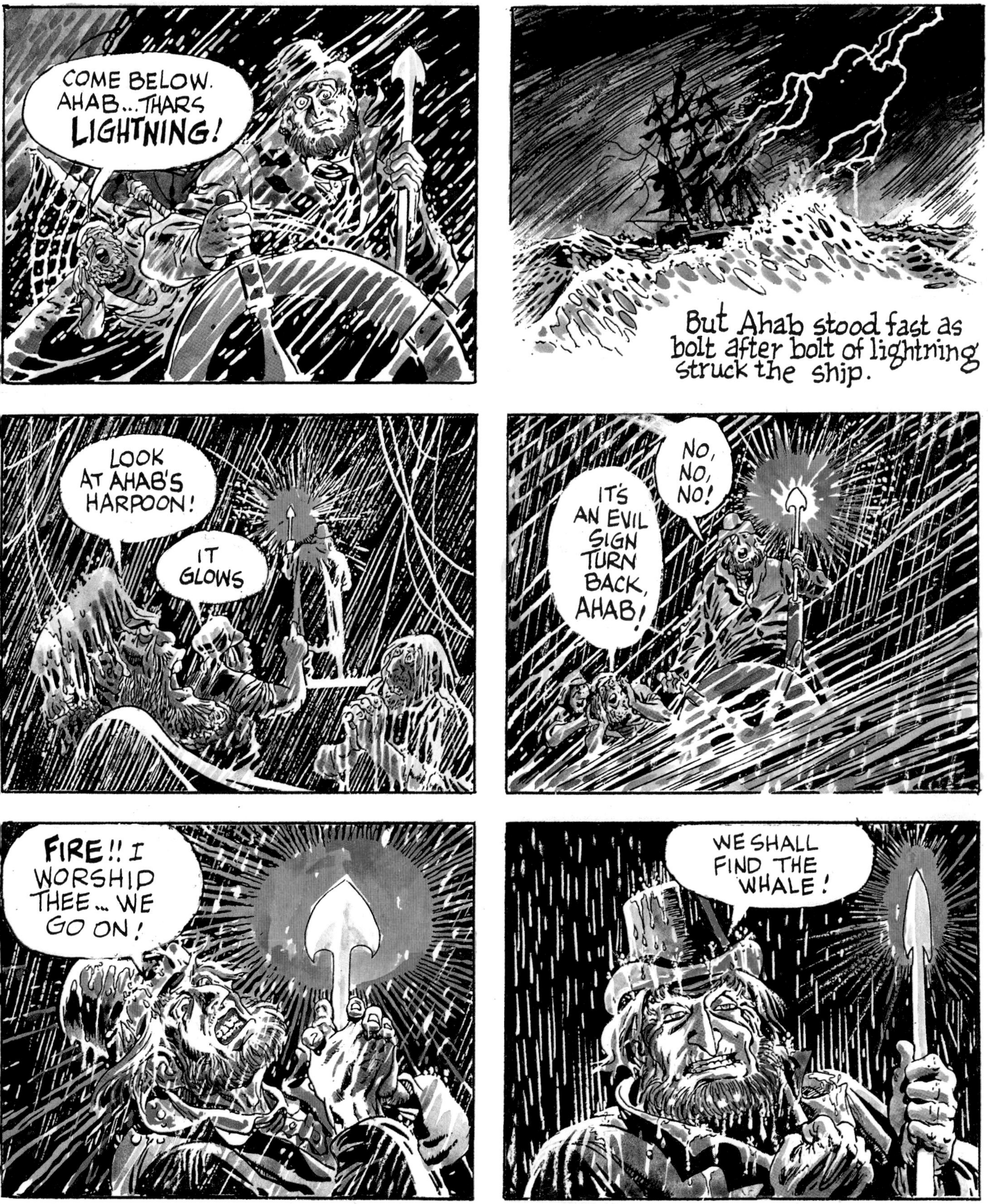
COME BELOW. AHAB... THARS LIGHTNING!
But Ahab stood fast as bolt after bolt of lightning struck the ship.
LOOK AT AHAB'S HARPOON!
IT GLOWS
NO, NO, NO!
IT'S AN EVIL SIGN TURN BACK, AHAB!
FIRE!! I WORSHIP THEE... WE GO ON!
WE SHALL FIND THE WHALE!

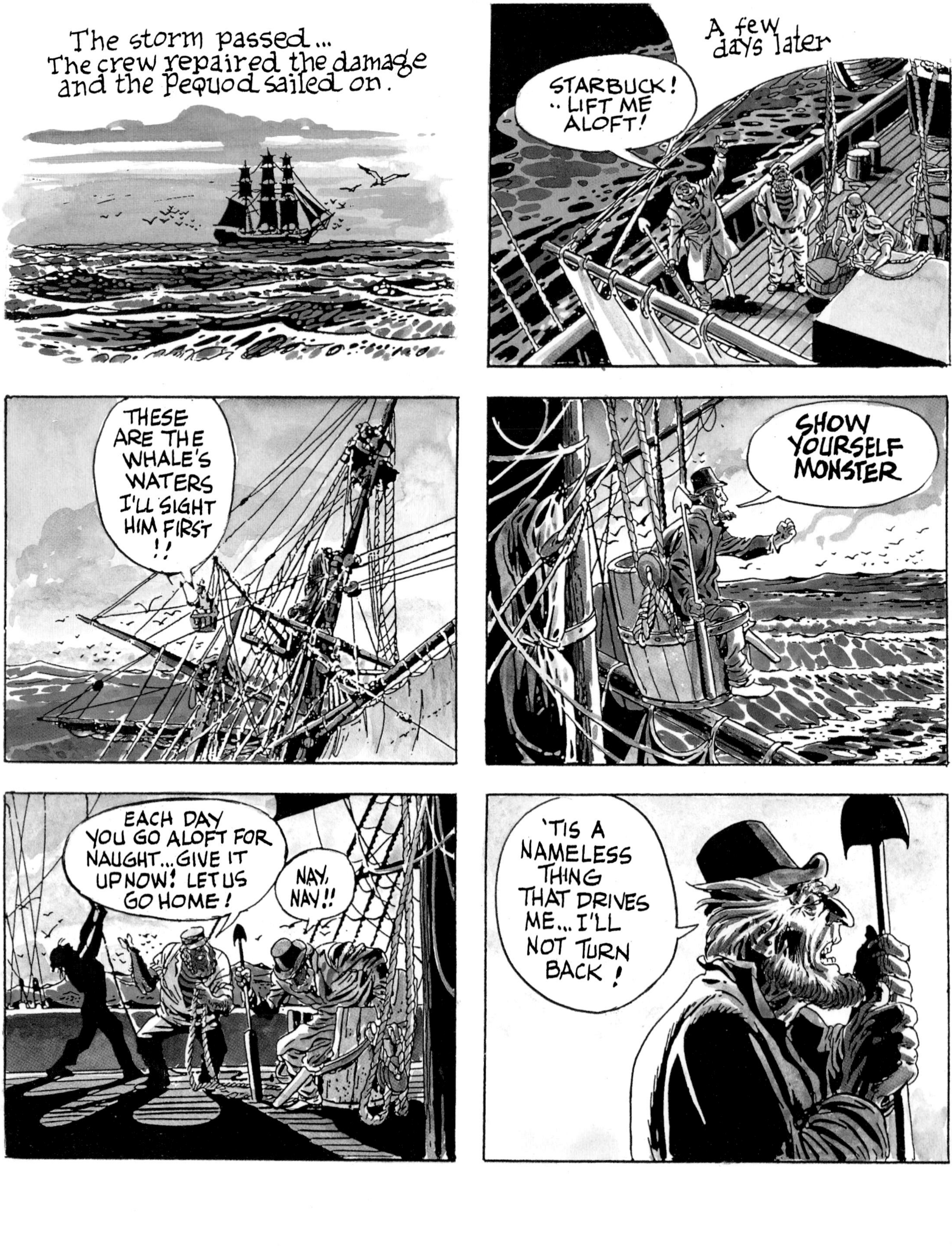
The storm passed...
The crew repaired the damage and the Pequod sailed on.
A few days later
STARBUCK! .. LIFT ME ALOFT!
THESE ARE THE WHALE'S WATERS I'LL SIGHT HIM FIRST!!
SHOW YOURSELF MONSTER
EACH DAY YOU GO ALOFT FOR NAUGHT...GIVE IT UP NOW! LET US GO HOME!
NAY, NAY!!
'TIS A NAMELESS THING THAT DRIVES ME... I'LL NOT TURN BACK!

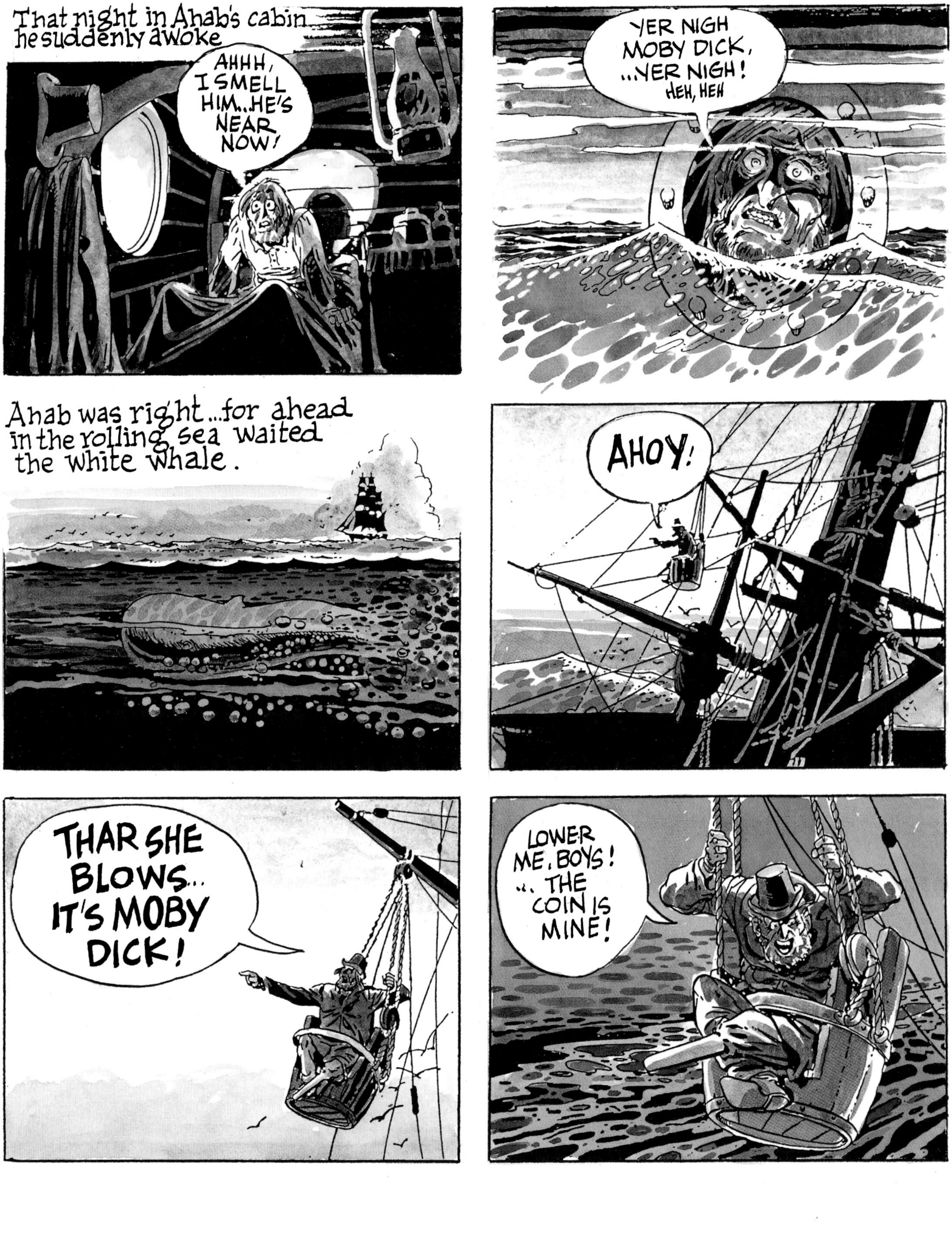

That night in Ahab's cabin he suddenly awoke
AHHH, I SMELL HIM..HE'S NEAR NOW!
YER NIGH MOBY DICK, ..YER NIGH! HEH, HEH
Ahab was right...for ahead in the rolling sea waited the white whale.
AHOY!
THAR SHE BLOWS... IT'S MOBY DICK!
LOWER ME, BOYS! .. THE COIN IS MINE!

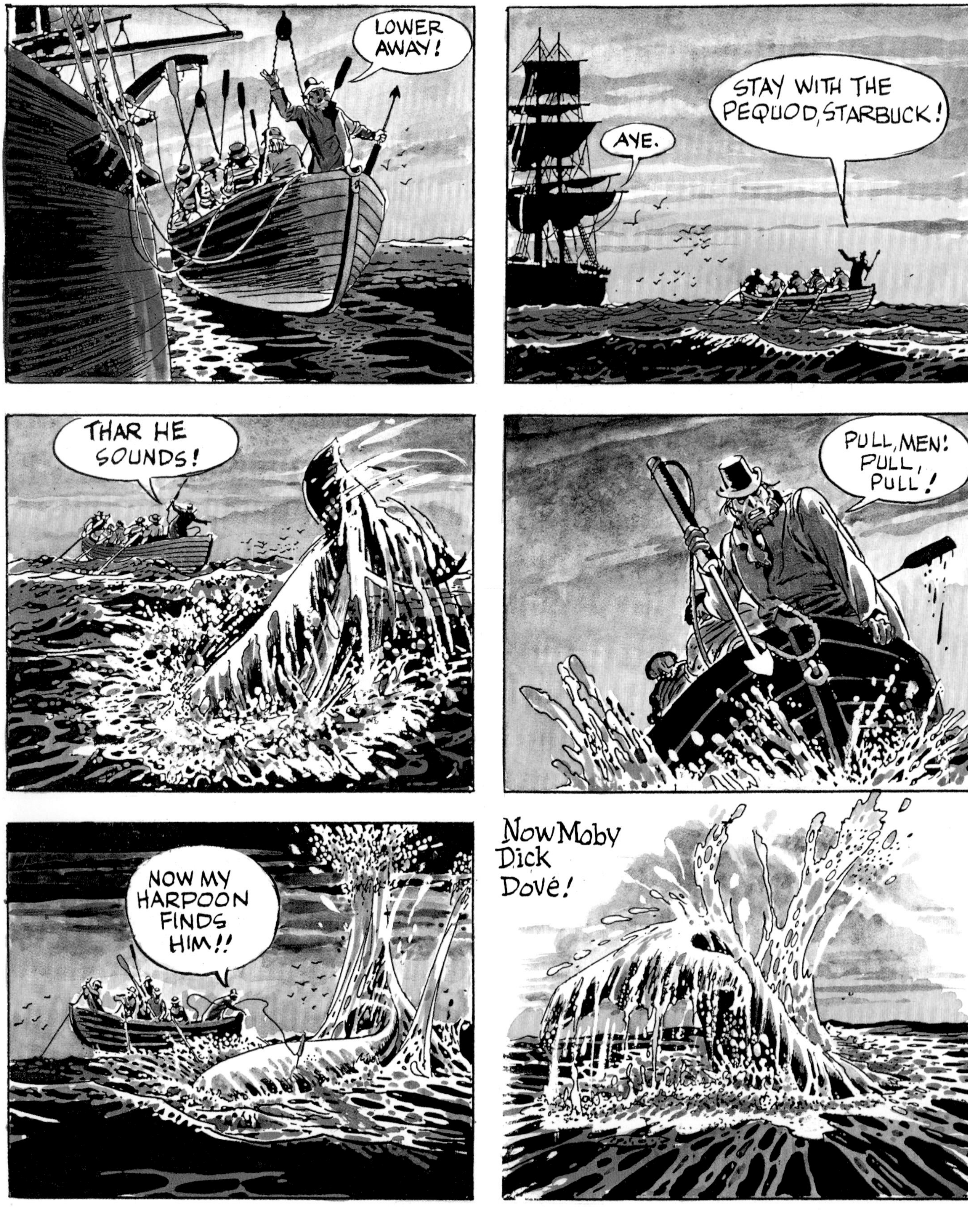
LOWER AWAY!
STAY WITH THE PEQUOD, STARBUCK!
AYE.
THAR HE SOUNDS!
PULL, MEN! PULL, PULL!
NOW MY HARPOON FINDS HIM!!
Now Moby Dick Dove!

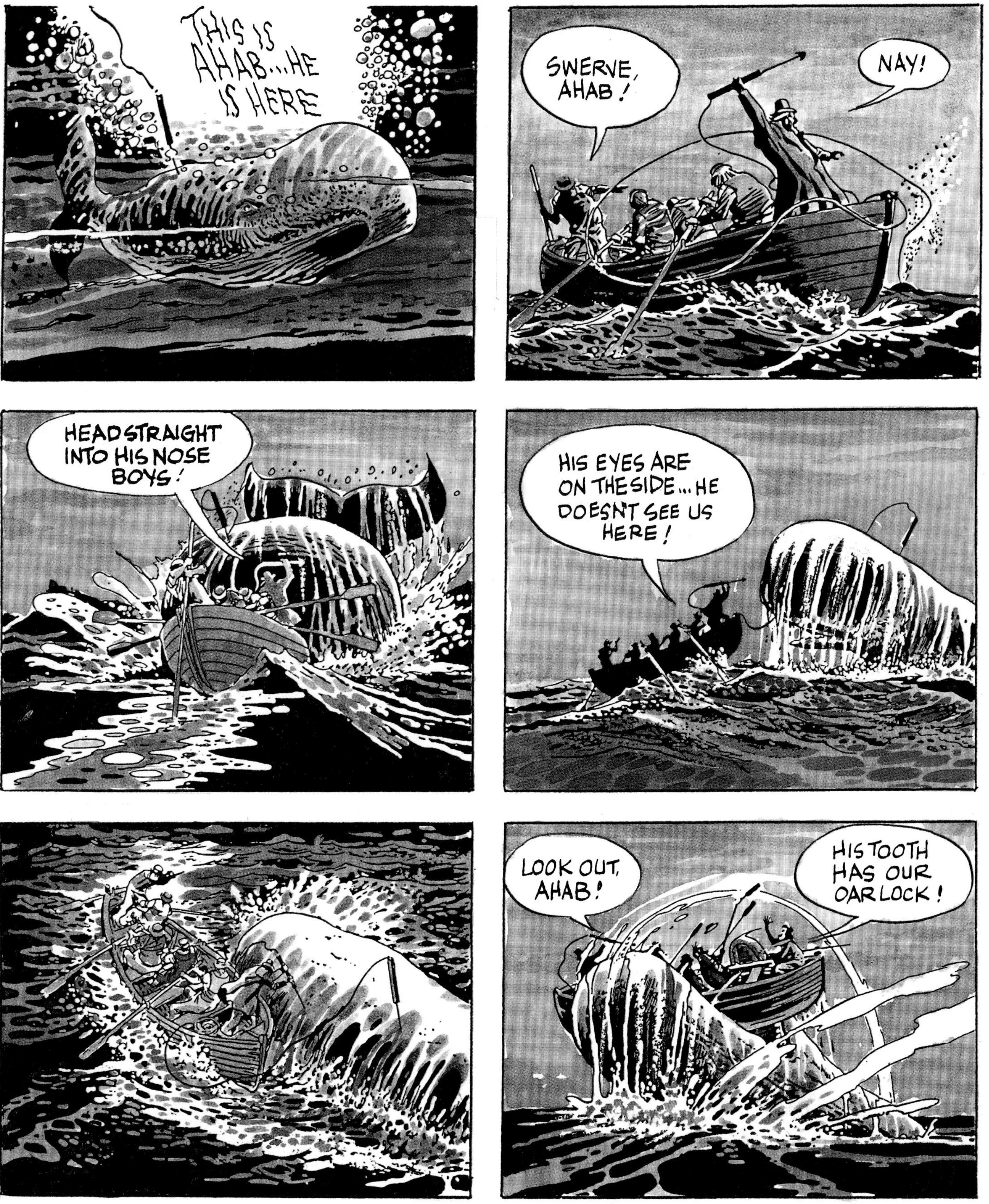
THIS IS AHAB... HE IS HERE
SWERVE, AHAB!
NAY!
HEAD STRAIGHT INTO HIS NOSE BOYS!
HIS EYES ARE ON THE SIDE... HE DOESN'T SEE US HERE!
LOOK OUT, AHAB!
HIS TOOTH HAS OUR OAR LOCK!

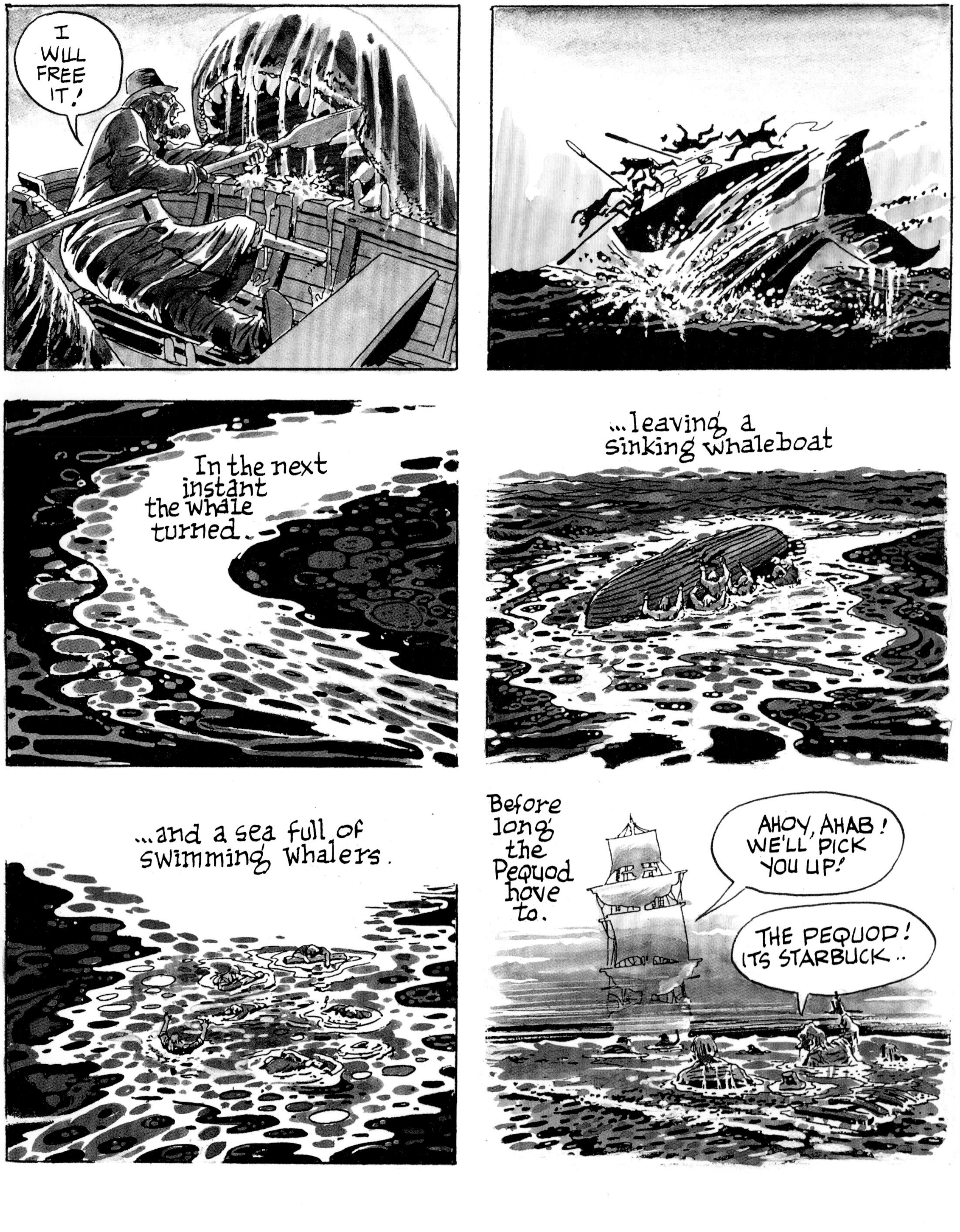
I WILL FREE IT!
In the next instant the whale turned..
...leaving a sinking whaleboat
...and a sea full of swimming whalers.
Before long the Pequod hove to.
AHOY, AHAB! WE'LL PICK YOU UP!
THE PEQUOD! ITS STARBUCK..

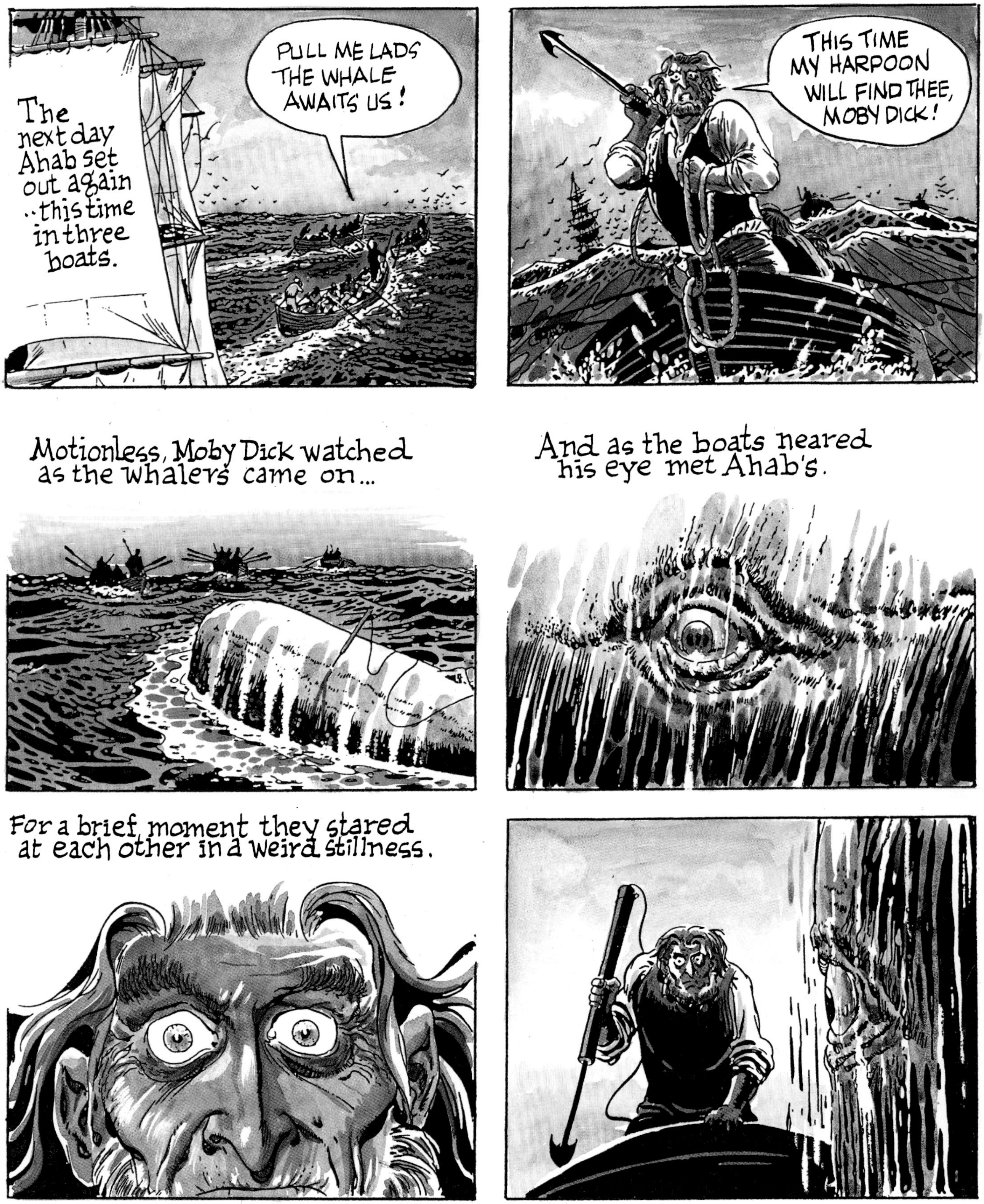
The next day Ahab set out again ..this time in three boats.
PULL ME LADS THE WHALE AWAITS US!
THIS TIME MY HARPOON WILL FIND THEE, MOBY DICK!
Motionless, Moby Dick watched as the whalers came on...
And as the boats neared his eye met Ahab's.
For a brief moment they stared at each other in a weird stillness.

Then in a flash his tail scattered the boats

Once more Moby Dick came to the surface.

Now Ahab's boat bore down on the whale

Ahab's harpoon found its mark. Moby Dick shuddered.

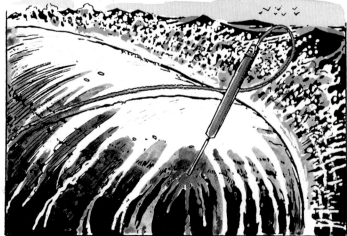

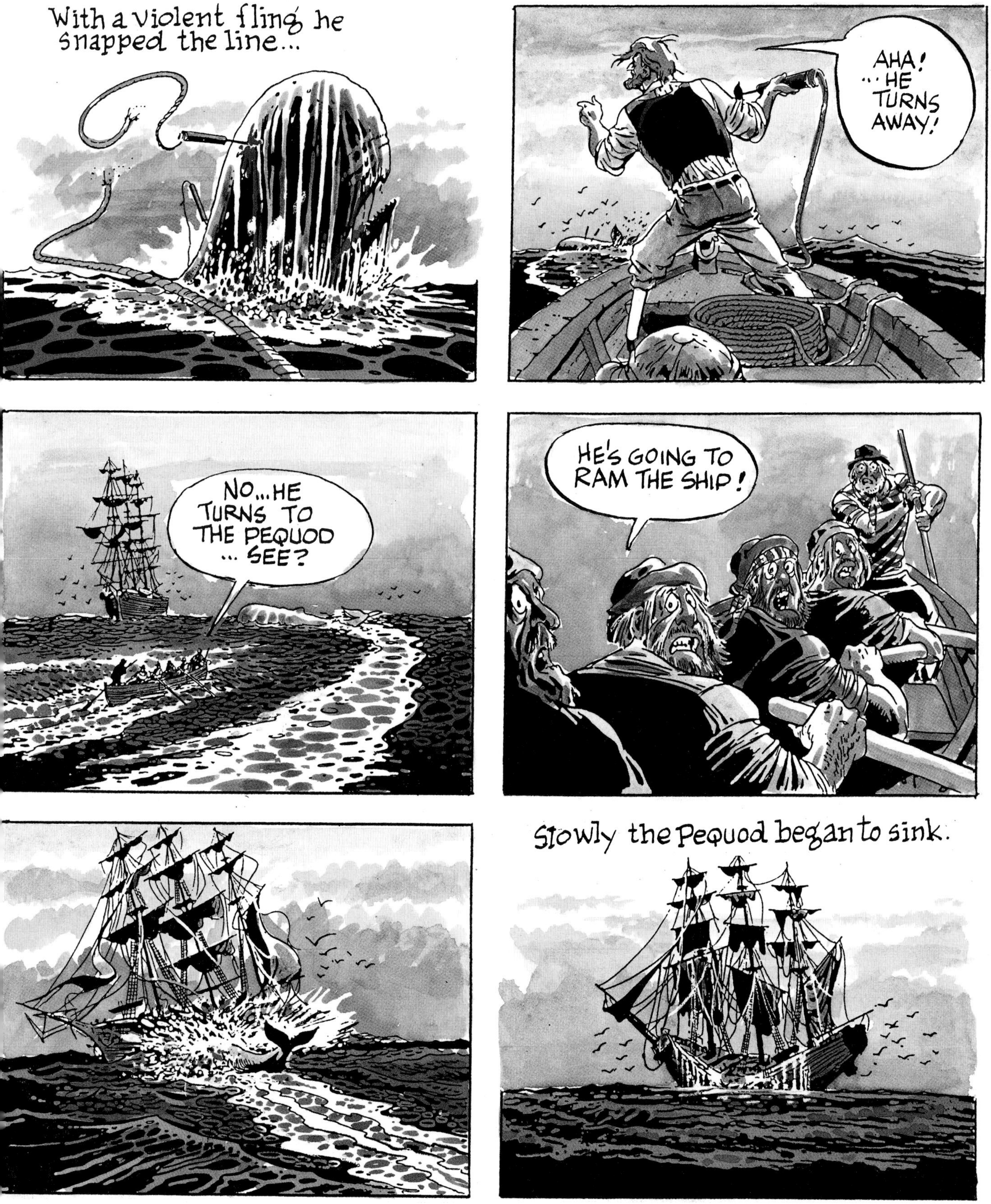
With a violent fling he snapped the line...
AHA! ...HE TURNS AWAY!
NO...HE TURNS TO THE PEQUOD ... SEE?
HE'S GOING TO RAM THE SHIP!
Slowly the Pequod began to sink.

But Ahab pursued the whale

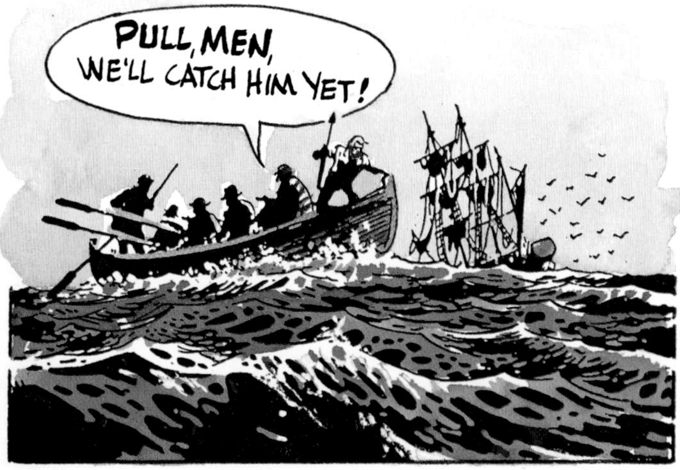
PULL, MEN, WE'LL CATCH HIM YET!

Now... slowly... they closed in on each other.

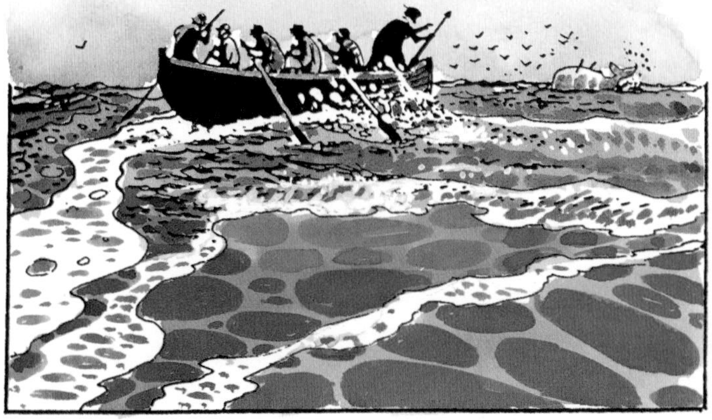

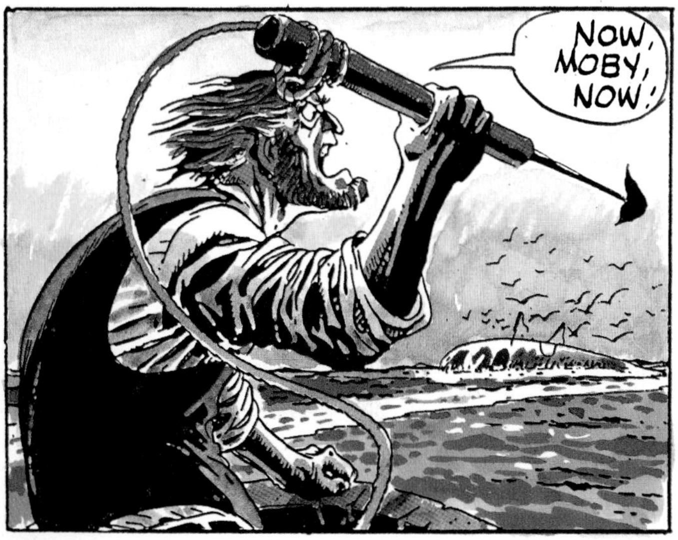
NOW, MOBY, NOW!

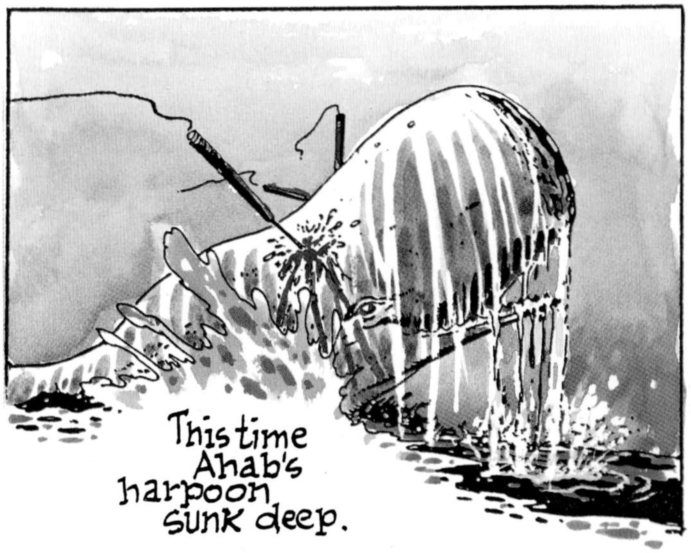
This time Ahab's harpoon sunk deep.

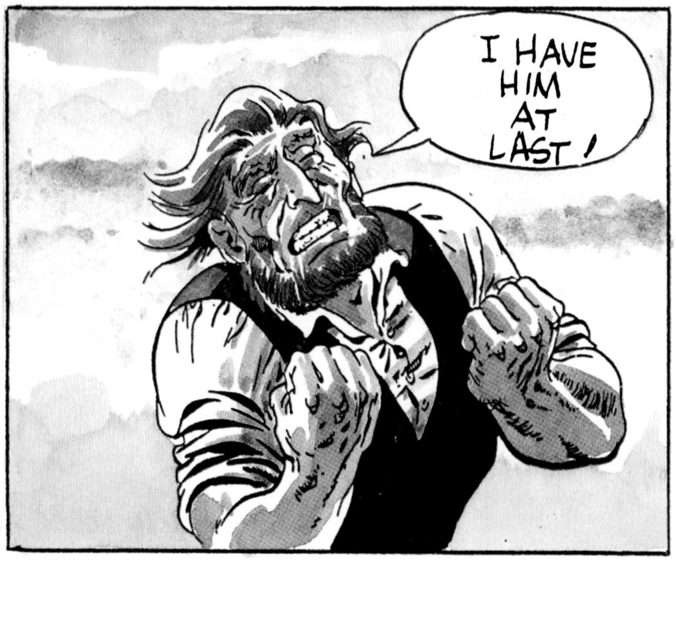
I HAVE HIM AT LAST!

Moby Dick turned pulling the harpoon and its line with him.

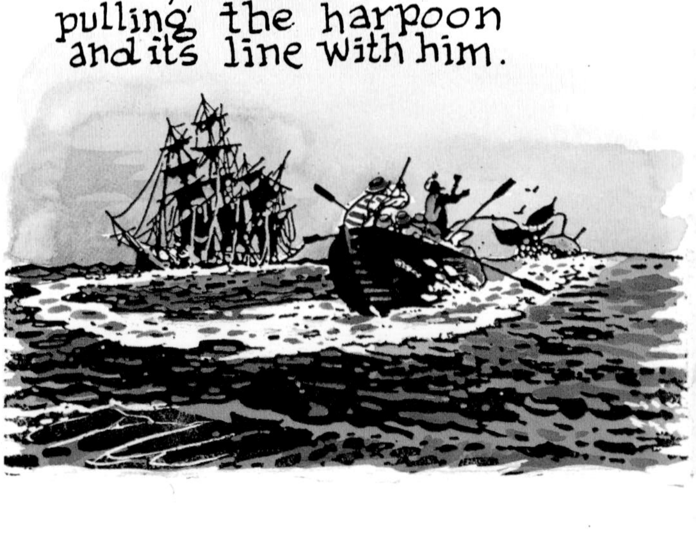

...the line
caught Ahab...

...and lifted him out of the boat
and into the sea...

...where Moby Dick
hauled him off...
into the watery
depths...

Then the sinking
Pequod finally went
down in a mighty
whirlpool.

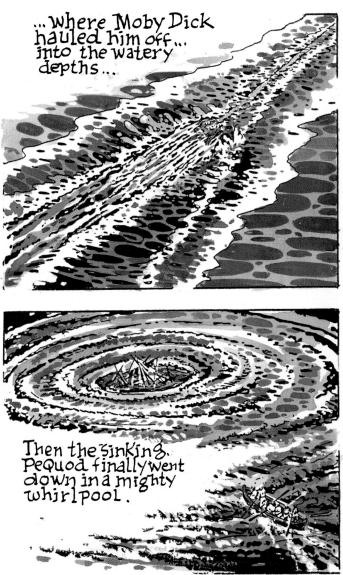

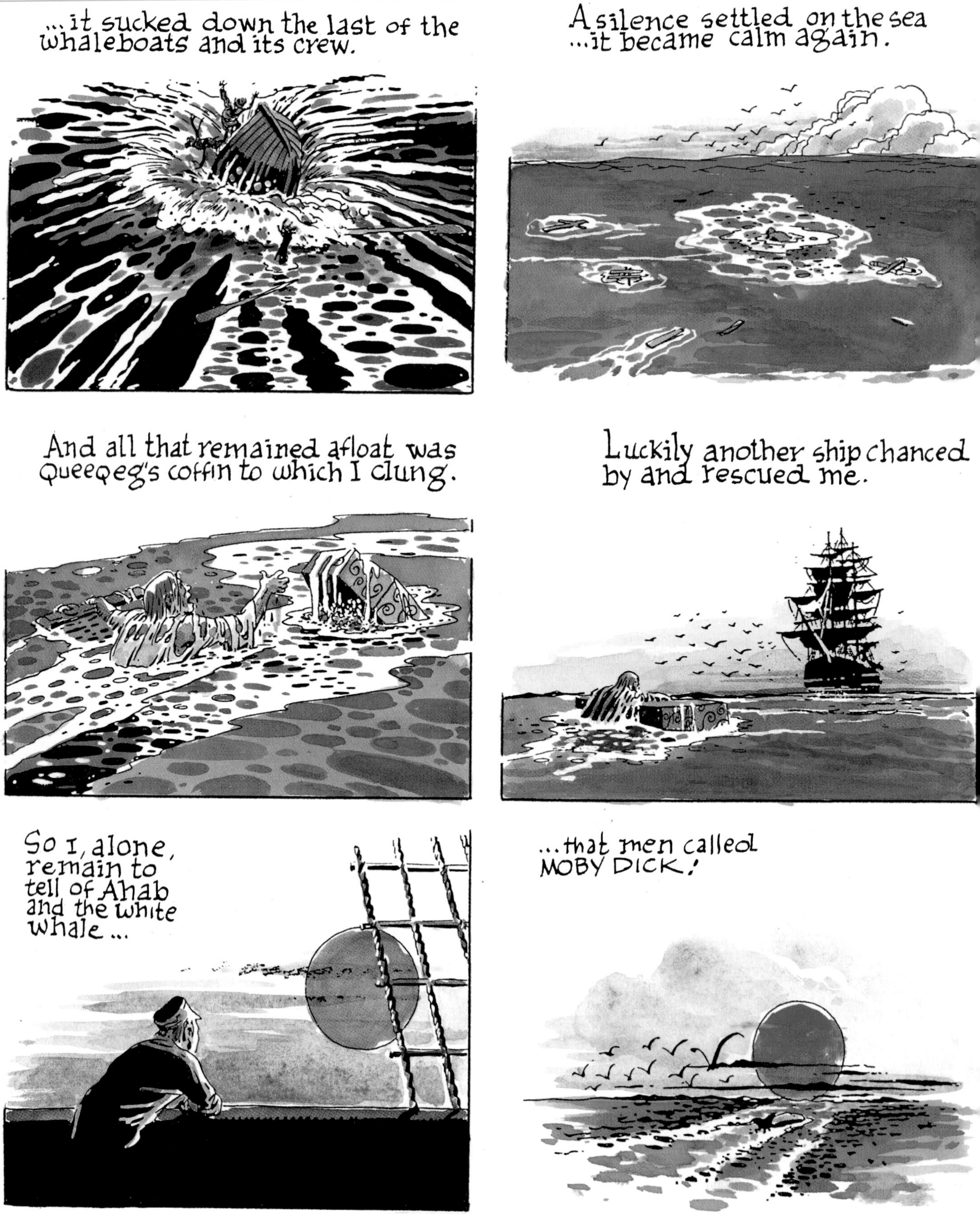
...it sucked down the last of the whaleboats and its crew.
A silence settled on the sea ...it became calm again.
And all that remained afloat was Queeqeg's coffin to which I clung.
Luckily another ship chanced by and rescued me.
So I, alone, remain to tell of Ahab and the white whale...
...that men called MOBY DICK!

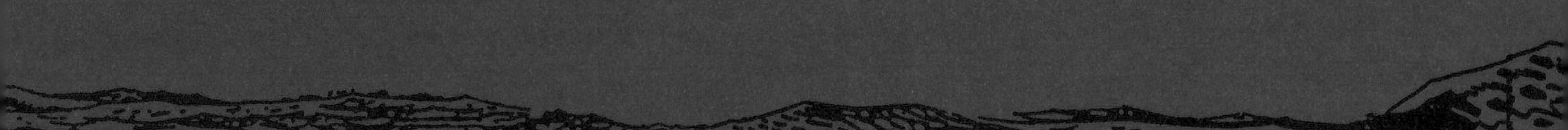